Harold's Heavenly Christmas

HAROLD'S HEAVENLY CHRISTMAS

a novel

Chris Whaley

NEW YORK

LONDON • NASHVILLE • MELBOURNE • VANCOUVER

HAROLD'S HEAVENLY CHRISTMAS

© 2021 Chris Whaley

Published in New York, New York, by Morgan James Publishing. Morgan James is a trademark of Morgan James, LLC. www.MorganJamesPublishing.com

Publisher's Note: This novel is a work of fiction. Names, characters, places, and incidents are either products of the author's imagination or used fictitiously. All characters are fictional, and any similarity to people living or dead is purely coincidental.

ISBN 9781631951688 paperback
ISBN 9781631951695 eBook
Library of Congress Control Number: 2020937554

Cover Design by:
Rachel Lopez
www.r2cdesign.com

Interior Design by:
Chris Treccani
www.3dogcreative.net

Morgan James is a proud partner of Habitat for Humanity Peninsula and Greater Williamsburg. Partners in building since 2006.

Get involved today! Visit
MorganJamesPublishing.com/giving-back

This book is dedicated to
Debbie Macomber.

I first heard of her in November 2013, when I was in
Canada for the filming of my book *The Masked Saint*.
Charged with the excitement of seeing my book come to
life on film, I had difficulty sleeping after being on the set
all day, so I looked for something to watch on television
and came across *Mrs. Miracle*. I saw it was based on
Debbie's book by the same title. I became an instant fan
and had to read all of her books.

Even though I'm an old professional wrestler, I have
a soft side and am hooked on the works of this great
author. Her writing captivates my mind and heart.

I hope you enjoy *Harold's Heavenly Christmas* and sense
the inspiration Debbie has had on my writing.

Thank you, Debbie, for your inspiration
and your kindness!

TABLE OF CONTENTS

CHAPTER ONE

Harold in Heaven

Christmas is a magical time. You really can't explain all the wonderful things that happen at this time of the year. As a matter of fact, sometimes the things that take place are downright heavenly. Such is the case with Harold.

It started as a normal call for Station 12, one of the busiest fire stations in the county. What seemed normal for the firefighters is nowhere close to what's normal for most people. Not only do they put out fires, they also deal with medical emergencies, including heart attacks.

Right when they were sitting down to eat a great meatloaf dinner, the alarm sounded at the station. All the firefighters did what they normally do. They dropped their forks and headed for the rescue car and the fire engine to take care of the call.

A cookout had gone bad. The backyard was on fire. The usual barbeque doesn't always cause any kind of an alarm, but when the firemen arrived on the scene, the fire had spread from the grill to the garage. The entire house was in danger.

All it takes for a fire to expand is the slightest carelessness. Still, these guys are professionals, and it didn't take long for them to get things under control and extinguish the fire.

It is amazing to watch professional firemen work. They do an incredible job. All of them work like a well-oiled, precise machine. But today, one of them was physically hurt.

By the end of the call, fifty-two-year-old Harold Longwood noticed some tightness in his chest and felt a little queasy. He was a veteran firefighter and close to retirement. He had been on thousands of calls like this one over his career. But he had never felt like this before.

Harold had treated many people who felt the way he now felt. He knew the signs and knew what needed to be done. But there is a bit of stubbornness in all of us that keeps us from acting when we should act. Harold kept his condition to himself, thinking it was not like other calls for people who felt as he felt then. He thought he was the exception to the rule. He believed he would feel better once he was back to the station.

But as the fire engine returned to the station, he was sweating profusely, his chest felt tighter, and he was in great discomfort. He reasoned he was overheated and just needed to lie down. He would be okay in a few minutes.

Back at the station, a paramedic noticed Harold was sweating and looking pale. Patrick made eye contact with another firefighter and nodded toward Harold. They both saw his discomfort and felt concerned.

Normally after a call, Harold would shower and change into a clean T-shirt and pants. Instead, he sat at the dinner table and put his head on the flat surface. All he needed was a little rest, just a minute or so. But now all the guys at the station realized Harold was not feeling well.

"Are you okay, man?" asked Buddy, the station lieutenant.

"Yeah. I'm okay. Just feeling my age, I guess."

"You look a little pale. Let me check your blood pressure," Buddy continued.

"No, I'll be okay!"

"That's not a request, Harold. Sit down and let me check your blood pressure," Buddy commanded.

This exchange brought concern from all the other guys. They took their cues from the lieutenant and went into action. One of them appeared with the equipment to check Harold's heart, while another took Harold's pulse.

"His pulse is high," Patrick reported.

Harold's blood pressure was also very high.

"I'm not taking any chances, Harold. You're EKG isn't normal. We're taking you to the ER to get you checked out."

Buddy was immediately on the radio, calling the battalion chief, Robert Hitchcock.

"Hey, Chief, Harold isn't looking so well. When we got back to the station after the barbeque fire, he kind of collapsed at the dinner table. He's pale and his vitals aren't normal. I think we should transport him to the ER."

The chief agreed, but Harold wasn't too happy with all the commotion. But Buddy and the chief outranked him. Harold didn't have a choice.

"Guys, you're making a big deal out of nothing. I'll be okay. Just let me rest a minute and eat my dinner."

Steve said, "Harold, we're your family in addition to being firefighters. And as your family, we aren't taking any chances. We're moving you to the ER."

The station did everything they were supposed to do, because they're professionals. Before Harold knew it, he was in the ER at Alderman General Hospital. Mario, Sanchez, Brian, Kevin, and the other guys said good-bye to him and told him they would be checking on him later.

Harold was amazed at how busy the ER was that day. As a firefighter-paramedic, he had seen a full ER, but today, it was unusually crowded. Even though he was hurting, he felt compassion for the people he saw waiting to be cared for.

Thankfully, the nurses moved Harold into one of the ER rooms. Sometimes, people have to wait for hours in the ER before they're treated, but when the problem involves the heart, everyone moves pretty quickly to get the patient into a room.

After a nurse informed a doctor about the fireman who was just brought in, the doctor made his way to Harold's room.

"Mr. Longwood, I'm Dr. Sessions. How are you feeling now?"

"I'm feeling a lot better, doctor. I'm feeling a lot better than I was."

"Tell me what happened," the doctor said, while he listened to Harold's heart with his stethoscope.

"Well, I was at work. I'm a firefighter, you know. And I was feeling a little light-headed. The guys took my blood pressure, and it was high, and some of my other vitals weren't looking so good. So they thought I better come in and get checked out. Better to be safe than sorry, I guess."

"Well, I'm going to hook up some monitors to you so we can see what's going on. Someone will be with you soon. And I agree, it's much better to be safe than sorry."

"Thanks, doc!" Harold said as the doctor left the room.

Harold scanned the antiseptic room and took a deep breath. He had never been in a situation like this before. He knew he hadn't been honest with the doctor. He really wasn't feeling better at all. His chest was tighter. Harold was a professional firefighter, but he was still a vulnerable human being. He didn't know what to do, so he did something he hadn't done in a while: he prayed as best he knew how.

"Well, God, I haven't talked to You like I should have. Especially with the line of work I'm in. I should talk to You more than I do. This was definitely a wake-up call. I sure hope You still remember me. This is Harold Longwood at the Alderman General."

Harold's left arm started to ache. He rubbed it as he continued talking to God, but he didn't notice his speech was becoming labored.

"I'm sorry God for the things I've done wrong. Please forgive me. I know I should have done some things differently. I can't believe I've waited this long to have a conversation with You."

The pain increased, but rather than call for help, Harold continued to talk with God.

"I've been listening to that Baptist preacher on TV at the station on Sundays. I believe what he said I need to do to go to heaven. I'm sorry . . ."

He collapsed on the bed and expelled his last breath.

With all that had been done right by his firefighter family, though he was in a hospital ER, his time came to leave this world. Nothing could change it.

Harold was on his way to heaven.

A moment later, a nurse entered the room to check on Harold. She had the equipment and monitors the doctor had ordered. She hummed as she began connecting the various devices to the still figure on the bed.

As she finished her task, she gently said, "Mr. Longwood? How are we doing? I've brought a couple of monitors for you."

When she set a monitor on the bed, she realized Harold wasn't breathing. She dropped the equipment and called out, "Code blue in 27! Code blue in 27!" She retrieved the defibrillator from the hallway and readied it for the doctor.

The doctor and several other nurses rushed in and began their resuscitation work, not knowing Harold already had one foot in heaven.

* * *

Harold thought he had closed his eyes for a moment and then opened them again. But things had changed drastically. He wasn't in the ER. He was in a very different place. Everything was white and serene. He heard a wonderfully pure voice.

"Hello, Harold. It's good to see you," a bearded man said as he placed his hands on the firefighter's shoulders.

Harold wasn't frightened but surprised. He looked at the man in front of him. He wore a white robe. The man looked almost angelic, and even though Harold was sure he had never met him, the man seemed familiar to him.

"Who are you?" Harold said as he cocked his head to one side.

"I'm Peter."

"Saint Peter?" Harold asked with a smile.

"Most people call me that, but I was a fisherman a long time before I got that handle," he said nonchalantly.

"So I must be in heaven. Is this heaven? I guess I didn't make it in the ER, huh? To be honest with you, I never liked that hospital. I guess those cutbacks at the hospital really didn't work."

"No, Harold, it wasn't the hospital's fault. It was your time. And I must tell you, you're in a lot better place than an emergency room."

"The last thing I remember is that I was praying," Harold said.

"And God heard your prayer, Harold!"

"What's next for me, Peter. I mean Saint Peter. What should I call you?"

"Peter is fine, Harold."

"I certainly don't mean any disrespect."

"None taken, Harold."

"Wow! This is so different! Can I fly? Wait, I don't have any wings! Is this like *It's a Wonderful Life,* and I have to earn my wings?"

"Harold, you've been watching too much TV at the fire station. But I must tell you, I love that movie, too! It's interesting you brought that up, because I do have an important assignment for you."

Harold looked a little stunned.

"An important assignment for me? I know you don't have a fire department up here. I was never very good at much else. But with the life I lived, you must have a cleanup job or something like that for me," he said and hung his head.

"No, Harold, nothing like that!" Peter said reassuringly.

"I really don't know much about the Bible or religious things. What could I possibly do?"

"You're going to help someone on earth who needs it."

"How can I do that? I'm dead!" Harold said in disbelief.

"Harold, you're more alive than you've ever been!" said Peter.

"But we're in heaven. Who in the world needs help up here?"

"You're going to help someone back on earth, Harold. Didn't you hear me?"

"How in the world am I going to do that?" Harold asked, scratching his head.

"You'll have everything you need. I'll be helping you as you help the person we're sending you to help."

"I'm confused. I can't imagine how this is going to work!"

"Harold, when we send you back to earth, the only people who will be able to see you will be the people we're sending you to help."

"But how will I know what to do? Do you have an instruction manual for me? I was never very good at following instructions. I know I'll mess this up. Are you sure you want me to do this?"

"Yes, Harold. Do you think we would send you unprepared for the task?"

"No. But, I . . . I just don't know!"

"That's okay. I understand Moses had some pretty good excuses on his first day too. When we send you down, *I'll* be helping you. You'll be able to hear my voice. I'll give you all the help you need to help the person you're supposed to help. You're going to do okay, Harold. Got it?"

"May I ask a question?" said Harold rather shyly.

"Sure."

"Why me? I mean why would you give an assignment like this to me?"

"Because, Harold, you're the perfect person to help him."

"Okay, then. I'm sure you need to fill me in on everything and let me watch him grow up and—"

"Like I said, this isn't *It's a Wonderful Life*. That's not how it works."

CHAPTER TWO
The Funeral

Bret had felt lonely before but never this lonely. The funeral home chapel wasn't very big, but it seemed huge with such a small number of people dispersed throughout the pews in the chapel. Bret sat silently on the front pew and stared at the casket.

He and his dad had not been that close over the last few years, but Bret loved his dad, and they occasionally communicated by phone. The news of his dad's passing had stunned him.

* * *

Ed Mills, the landlord at Pine Woods, was concerned when he didn't see John Davidson for a couple of days and figured he might be sick. When John didn't show up for work and when no one answered the phone, his boss knew something was wrong. John had never missed work and never called in sick. The boss decided to make a call to be sure. He called 911.

"911, what's your emergency?"

"I'm not sure but I'd rather be safe than sorry."

"Sir?" the 911 operator replied.

"Well, one of my employees hasn't shown up for work, and it's not like him. Is there any way an officer can go by and check on him?"

"What's the address, sir?"

A short time later a patrolman knocked on the landlord's door.

"We've had a call about the guy in 2B. I need you to get the key and take me to his apartment."

"Okay, no problem. To be honest, I'm a little worried about him myself. I haven't seen him out all weekend. To tell you the truth, I was planning to check on him myself. I'll get the key."

When no one answered the door, the landlord opened it.

"Mr. Davidson . . . this is Officer Grant. May we come in?"

"Hey, John, you there?" the landlord called out.

A few minutes later their worst fears were realized. The landlord and the officer found John Davidson in bed. Evidently, he had died in his sleep.

The landlord had never made a call like the one he was about to make. But he was the best candidate to call Bret and let him know his dad had passed.

"Bret, this is Ed Mills, your dad's landlord. I'm afraid I've got some pretty bad news. Your dad has passed away."

Bret silently listened to the Ed. He had never even thought about the day he would hear this kind of news.

"Bret? . . . Bret? . . . Are you there?"

"Yes, Mr. Mills. How did he die?"

"It looks like he passed away in his sleep. Your dad's boss got worried when he didn't show up, and when he didn't call in, he called the police. I was concerned, too, when I didn't see him all weekend. He's been going to church the last couple of months, and I didn't see his car move at all last Sunday. I'm very sorry, Bret. Your dad was a great guy."

"Yes. Yes, he was. Thank you, Mr. Mills."

* * *

Now Bret sat alone in the chapel, reminiscing about his parents. His mom had died in an automobile accident years ago. His dad never remarried.

A few people occasionally walked up to Bret and offered a hand and condolences, but nothing they said seemed to break his trance. Bret was alone now, with no relatives and very few friends. The only lights at the end of the tunnel were Angie, his fiancée, and the job he enjoyed.

Bret looked at his watch as the time approached for the service to begin. *Where was Angie?* He looked to the back of the chapel only to see the funeral director checking his watch. Something happened and he felt a rush over his body. Angie was probably caught in traffic, he reasoned. Then he looked at his phone. No messages.

The funeral director tapped him on the shoulder and said the service would be starting in a couple of minutes. His father's pastor was there, and he would officiate the service. Again Bret checked his watch and cell phone. He nodded neglectfully that it was okay to begin.

Bret had met Pastor McDowell before but knew very little about him. He remembered the day his dad called to tell him about what had happened in his life.

* * *

"Bret, this is dad. How're you doing?"

"Oh, I'm fine, dad. How about you?"

"I'm probably better than I've ever been in all my life."

"Really? What'd you do? Hit the lottery?"

John Davidson chuckled a little. "No, nothing like that. I was at the mall the other day, just sitting on a bench and sipping a coffee. A man sat down next to me. He was waiting on his wife and daughters."

"Did he give you a million dollars?" Bret teased.

"No. Anyway, we started talking, what we did for a living. You know, the usual chitchat."

"Yeah, I gotcha. Dad, is this going to take long? I've got something to do."

"No, it's not long, son. Please, let me share this with you."

"Okay, Dad. I'm sorry for rushing you."

"That's okay. Well, the guy is a preacher. I really enjoyed talking with him. So I started going to his church. I've been going a couple of weeks now. It's great. I'm really enjoying it. I don't think I've ever felt this great about life ever."

"That's wonderful, Dad. I'm happy for you."

"I was wondering if you might go with me this Sunday."

"No, Dad. I'm sorry. I've got a really busy weekend coming up."

"Maybe next week?" John said with a hint of guilt.

"I'll get back to you on that, Dad."

But he never did. Though he actually met the pastor by chance. Bret had stopped by his dad's place to pick up something. They talked for a short time before Bret made his exit. But at least they had met.

* * *

Pastor McDowell approached the podium and put his Bible and notes in order as he made eye contact with Bret. He smiled and cleared his throat and began.

"We're here today to honor a great man: John Michael Davidson. He was born on August 7, 1954 and graduated from this life just three days ago, on December 7."

Bret looked down at the bulletin the funeral home had provided. It had his dad's name and birth date and the date of his passing on one side and Psalm 23 on the other.

"John and I met at the mall and chatted over coffee. It was my pleasure to lead him to our Savior, Jesus Christ. John had a great desire to know more about the Lord and to serve Him the rest of his days. John found purpose in his life and was someone you can be very proud of, Bret," the pastor said, searching for the son's eyes.

The service seemed both long and short to Bret, and then he heard the pastor give a benediction. It seemed long because he couldn't understand why Angie wasn't beside him. It seemed short because there were so many things Bret thought of that he wished he had said to his dad. But life never gives us any warnings about how much time we have with each other.

John Davidson had served in Vietnam, but he had never said anything about that time to Bret. So it felt a little odd when the funeral director handed the folded flag to Bret at the graveside service.

Bret stood and looked at the casket one more time. As he turned around, the pastor took his hand. "I'm so sorry for your loss. If there is ever anything I can do for you to be of help, please don't hesitate to call on me. And Bret, I really mean that. Here's my card. It has my cell number on it."

"Thank you, pastor. Dad really thought a lot of you. Thank you for all you did for him."

Bret walked slowly toward his car. When he turned around, his mind was full of memories, a flurry of mental images. It seemed like a movie as he remembered his dad running alongside him, encouraging him as he rode his bike for the first time. He could see his dad's face in the stands as he walked up to the plate in Little League. He smiled at the memory of his parents hugging each other when his name was called at his high school graduation ceremony.

He got into his car and drove out of the cemetery. Tears finally rolled down his cheeks. The reality of his dad's death finally hit him. And concern about Angie not being at the funeral was tying a knot in his stomach.

Chapter Three
The Boss

"The economy isn't getting any better, Mr. Glassman. We're not in terrible shape. In fact, we're still making a good profit. Just not what you're used to," said Bill McCarty, the chief financial officer of Glassman Industries.

That might be good news to most company owners, but Arnold Glassman thought McCarty was one of those guys who gave you the willies whenever you had to talk to him. To be honest, there weren't many who liked Bill McCarty. He showed no compassion for anyone. He seemed to have a heart of stone. Most of the people at the company couldn't understand how a guy like McCarty could make it without getting punched in the face all the time. In fact, a lot of people would avoid him whenever they saw him in the hallway rather than have to say anything to him. Even

19

if they did say something to him, he seldom replied. If he did answer, it was more a grunt than a word.

"Given the market conditions, however, I suggest a fifteen percent cutback in payroll. That should put your profit margin back to what you're expecting. When the economy comes back, we can rehire the layoffs or seek more qualified candidates. I really don't see why we can't limp a little with fewer employees until this thing turns around."

* * *

Arnold Glassman was sixty years old and had a strong reputation as a solid businessman and a good man. He had built his company from the ground up. But as much as he loved his company, nothing came close to love he had for his daughter, his only child. And since she was his only remaining family, he loved her more than life itself.

As a businessman, Arnold had known some difficult years during the life of his company. But the current economy was making him more than a little uncomfortable.

No one had given Arnold anything; he worked for everything he had. He had no formal training or college background. He went to work as soon as he graduated high school. But Arnold had a head for business and worked tirelessly to make his company a reality.

Lately, though, he hadn't been feeling well. A couple of months ago he noticed he was short of breath and even wheezing a little. He thought it might be a cold or the flu. His administrative assistant suggested several times he see a doctor, but Arnold was sure whatever it was, it would quickly pass. Gradually, however, the wheezing turned into a racking cough.

Now, during this meeting with McCarty, Arnold had another coughing spell. His face reddened as he tried to catch his breath.

"Are you all right, Mr. Glassman?" McCarty asked.

"I'm okay," Arnold said as he tried to catch his breath. "This cold has been dogging me for weeks. Or maybe it's the flu."

McCarty awkwardly covered his mouth with a handkerchief.

Arnold's cough calmed, and he said, "I'm seeing a doctor this afternoon. I've held off on that for too long. Hopefully he'll clear this all up."

He looked back at McCarty's spreadsheets, charts, and graphs, but his wheezing and coughing wouldn't let him concentrate. He dropped everything on his desk and looked at the CFO.

"If that's what we have to do, Billy, to get things moving, then do it. I want HR to work closely with you on the layoffs. Make sure we only weed out the less essential ones."

"I'll take care of it, Mr. Glassman. And I hope you feel better very soon."

"Yes, yes. I'm sure I will," Arnold said as he tried to focus on the proposal papers again.

As the CFO began to leave the office, another coughing spell hit Arnold. He coughed into his handkerchief until he finally got his breath back. But his sense of relief was short-lived when he saw a crimson stain in the handkerchief.

He sat back in his chair, shocked. His face went pale as he pondered what this might mean—what this meant about his health. He called for his assistant.

"Mrs. DeBarry, what time is my appointment this afternoon?"

"It's at 3:30, Mr. Glassman. And your daughter is on line one."

Arnold took a breath and paused before picking up the phone.

"How's my baby girl?" he said with a wheeze.

"Will I ever be anything but your baby girl," twenty-eight-year-old Kacie teased her dad.

"You'll always be my baby girl," he said as a smile spread across his face. "How are you doing, sweetheart?"

"I'm fine, Dad. I was just wondering if we could have a late lunch. It's a teacher workday, so I'm free if you are."

"Normally I would, honey. But I've got a very important meeting at 3:30. How about supper? Could we do that around six at our favorite place?"

"That sounds great, Dad. I'll see you there! Good luck with your meeting."

"Okay, baby. I'll meet you there!"

Arnold sat back and took a deep breath as his eye fell on Kacie's photo on his desk. He had given up hoping she might one day take over the business. He understood her dream was to be a schoolteacher.

She was everything to him, and he was everything to her. Eleanor, Kacie's mom, and Arnold had divorced when their daughter was too little to know what was happening. His heart had shattered when he learned Eleanor had been unfaithful. The affair turned his world upside down. But Arnold pursued custody of Kacie, and Eleanor didn't contest it. In fact, she moved across the country and never showed any interest in Kacie's life after that. But Kacie healed her father's heart, and the two were devoted to each other.

"Mr. Glassman. Mr. Glassman!" Mrs. DeBarry called from the door, interrupting his thoughts.

Arnold shook his head, "Yes, what is it?"

"Ed Swartz from shipping would like a few minutes, if it's okay with you. I can schedule an appointment tomorrow if you want."

"No, no need. Send him in," Arnold said and tried to stifle another cough.

"Thank you for seeing me, Mr. Glassman. I'll not take up much of your time."

"What is it, Ed? Everything okay in shipping?" Arnold asked as he put his handkerchief in his pocket.

"We always have a few difficulties, as you might expect. But I can handle them."

"Well, what is it?" Arnold said, hearing a little annoyance in his own voice.

"Mr. Glassman, I don't agree with Bill McCarty's decisions. If I can be completely honest, he's a bit of a bloodsucking, heartless, non-caring south end of a northbound horse."

Arnold chuckled a little as he looked over the CFO's earlier presentation.

"Ed, we're running into a little bit of a hard time. Billy's going to get us through it. I'll take your criticism into consideration. But let's see how the next couple of weeks go, okay?"

"You're the boss, Mr. Glassman. I just wanted to go on record that I'm not a fan of all his proposed cutbacks."

"Thank you, Ed. And thank you for the great job you've always done for me."

"You're welcome, sir," the head of shipping said as he left the office.

Arnold leaned back and looked at Kacie's picture. His cough started back up.

Chapter Four
The Breakup

Angie, this is Bret. I'm worried about you. Please call me." He put his cell phone down and immediately it rang. He looked at it and saw it was Angie. He quickly answered.

"Angie! Are you okay?"

"Yes," she said. "I'm fine."

"I was so worried when you weren't at the funeral. What happened?"

"Are you home?" Angie asked with some hesitation in her voice.

"Yes."

"Could we meet at O'Donnell's at six?"

"Okay, babe. I'll be there."

"I'll see you soon, Bret."

Angie never said good-bye; she ended the call abruptly.

Still, Bret thought she sounded strange. Maybe she was embarrassed about not making the funeral. He tried to imagine what might have happened. Did she have some kind of phobia about funerals? Maybe she'd had a bad childhood experience at a funeral. Maybe her car wouldn't start. Maybe she just got sick. Well, he'd find out soon enough.

He sat back on the couch, pulled a photo album off the coffee table, and began looking at pictures of him and his dad, his mom and dad, and him and Angie.

Bret had met Angie through a friend. Normally he never attended parties—they were boring and he had better ways of spending his time. But he had very few friends, and the party was a chance to increase that number. So he went.

At first, everything was as he expected. He felt he was alone on an island. Occasionally someone said, "Hi," but that was it. He felt increasingly uncomfortable and thought he'd leave while the night was still young.

Then his eyes fell on a beautiful woman who looked to be as alone as he felt. His pulse quickened at the thought of introducing himself. Then another woman approached her, but that conversation ended quickly and she was alone again.

He convinced himself he had nothing to lose and nervously walked toward her.

"Hi, I'm Bret Davidson."

"I'm Angie Harrison," she smiled and made eye contact.

"I saw you from across the room and noticed you looked almost as uncomfortable as I was feeling."

"Does it show that much?" Angie asked with a twinkle in her eye.

"I usually avoid parties because I don't know a lot of people," Bret said with a twinge of embarrassment.

Was this too much information? Were his words coming out all right? He even wondered if she might be rating his grammar. Did she notice how nervous he was?

"Me too," she said, which made him relax a little.

"What do you do for a living?" Bret asked.

"Oh, I'm a paralegal for Martin and Martin."

"Glad I didn't start out with a lawyer joke," he said with a chuckle.

"I'm sure I've heard most of them," she said. "You should hear the ones paralegals tell."

That was the beginning of what Bret felt was a potential relationship. They made plans to meet for dinner the next night. And they continued seeing each other. A year later, Bret proposed and Angie accepted. They were planning to set a date and talk about the wedding. From Bret's point of view, everything was great. And then he heard that his father had died.

* * *

As the sun began to set, Bret entered the restaurant and looked for Angie.

"May I help you?" the hostess asked.

"I'm meeting someone. I don't know if she's already here or not," he said as he scanned the tables. Then he saw Angie wave from the back of the restaurant.

"There she is," Bret said and made his way toward her.

As good as it was to see her, he was a little taken back when he reached the table, and she didn't get up to give him a hug. That was peculiar, especially since he'd buried his dad that afternoon, and she hadn't show up for the funeral. Still, he leaned over, kissed her cheek, and took the seat next to her.

"Bret, I'm . . . I really didn't mean to—"

She seemed frustrated. Obviously, she was embarrassed about her absence.

He tried to help, so he asked, "Were you tied up in traffic?"

"No," she said and looked down at the table.

"Oh. Well, what happened?"

"Bret, I just didn't want to go. I don't like funerals. I didn't know your dad that much. And funerals creep me out. I was trying to tell you that yesterday, but you just didn't hear me."

"I'm sorry, but, honey, as I'm sure you can imagine, I was pretty distraught yesterday. I'm sure I missed a lot of what you were saying. Surely you can understand that."

Angie continued to look at the table.

Then it hit him. She hadn't been making eye contact with him lately. Early on in their relationship, she had made great eye contact. Funny how he hadn't noticed until now, once that had changed.

"Well, the funeral is old news. It was difficult for me. And I missed having you by my side. But I understand. Some things creep me out, too," he said, trying to find common ground and also give her some encouragement.

"Bret . . . we need to talk," she said, not lifting her head.

He immediately had a sick feeling in his stomach. Those four words were notorious. This didn't sound good at all.

"Sure, honey. What's on your mind? I'm sure we're going to have to make some adjustments after we're married about things like this. But the good news is that I don't have any other relatives. So you won't have to go to any more funerals."

"That's not it," she said.

Then she looked him in the eye. But this wasn't a good look. Usually, he saw a connection with her whenever their eyes met. Now, she looked at him, and there was no kind of connection between them.

"What is it?"

"I don't want to . . . I mean . . . I can't . . . I can't marry you, Bret."

"What?" he said as he tried to take her hand.

She put her hands in her lap.

"Bret, I've been doing a lot of thinking and soul-searching. I don't love you. I mean, I really like you and care for you. You're a real sweet guy . . . But I can't marry you."

He felt an actual pain in his heart. His mind went blank. He looked down at the table and closed his eyes.

"Bret, I'm sorry. But I can't go through with something I know isn't right."

He struggled for words, but all he could say was, "Did the funeral make you feel this way?"

"No, I've been coping with this for a couple of months."

Bret realized she had stopped making eye contact with him that long.

"What if we take some time? Maybe counseling?" he asked, trying to find something to say that would end the pain in his chest, stop his world from spinning.

"No," Angie said before he could say anything more. "No, Bret. I don't need to take any more time to think this thing over. I'm sorry about the timing, but I can't continue putting up a front about loving you. I just don't love you."

She slowly took off the engagement ring and gave it back to Bret. She leaned over and kissed his cheek, picked up her purse, and said, "I'm really sorry, Bret. I wish you nothing but the best."

"No, Angie. Please sit down. Give me a moment. You owe me that much."

Reluctantly, she sat down, rolling her eyes as she placed her purse on the table.

"Something started this. What was it?"

"Bret, what kind of a life, what kind of a future can we have with your job at Glassman's? In a year's time, you haven't gotten a single raise. I've had two raises this past year."

"It's my job?" Bret said, disgust in his voice.

"No, not just the job. You never look at the future. I'm motivated. I want nice things. I want to travel. There are so many things I want to do. We're so different," she said, looking frustrated.

"I look at the future. I saw a future of growing old with the woman I loved. I saw a future with children. I saw a great future. Things are nice, traveling is great, but having someone you love by your side is more important than all those other things."

"Bret, we're too different. It would never work. I'm sorry."

This time, she didn't kiss his cheek as she picked up her purse and walked away.

"And the hits just keep on coming," Bret thought as he looked down at the table. "First, my dad. Now, my fiancée. What else can possibly happen to make this day any worse?"

Bret put the engagement ring in his pocket and stared at the table. He closed his eyes. Even in the worst moments of his life, he had never experienced anything like this. He didn't notice the server trying to get his attention.

"Welcome to O'Donnell's. May I take your drink order?" said the smiling waitress.

"No. I'm sorry. I've won't be staying," he said as he got up.

After getting into his car, he just stared ahead for a while. Finally he turned the key, backed out, and started home. But he couldn't focus on driving. He didn't realize he was slowing down until the driver behind him honked his horn.

Bret concentrated on the road ahead of him. If he could make it home, he'd try to put all of this into some kind of perspective.

CHAPTER FIVE
Bad News

Arnold Glassman was not a man accustomed to waiting. He tried to look at the magazines in the waiting room, but nothing caught his attention. He looked at his phone to see if anyone had called. No calls.

He was not used to being nervous. He usually made other people nervous. He was a wealthy, powerful man. But now he was nervous. He was anxious about what the doctor would find. What would he do if the news were bad?

"Mr. Glassman," called the nurse.

"Yes," he said.

"Please follow me," she said.

Arnold walked into the room. He never liked examining rooms, even when it was just a normal checkup.

He certainly didn't like it when there was a possibility of something being drastically wrong with him.

"The doctor will be with you soon. Please unbutton your shirt and have a seat," the nurse said as she closed the door.

Again, Arnold found himself in an uncomfortable waiting mode. This was no better than the waiting room. He looked for a magazine but there were none. He looked at the doctor's credentials on wall. A graduate of the University of Michigan medical school. And board certified, whatever that meant.

"Mr. Glassman, how are you today?" the doctor said as he walked in and placed Arnold's file on the table.

"Well, obviously, not well if I'm here," Arnold said with a little venom in his voice.

"What seems to be wrong?"

"Well, I've been coughing and wheezing real bad. And earlier today, when I was coughing, I had a bloody discharge in my handkerchief."

The doctor placed his stethoscope on Arnold's chest and asked him to breathe. Arnold took a couple of deep breaths and started coughing. He coughed as he had earlier in the day. The doctor handed him a tissue and asked him to cough into it. And just as earlier in the day, there was a bloody discharge.

The doctor examined the discharge and then scraped it into a container and placed a lid on it.

"I'm going to schedule a blood test and also an MRI for as soon as possible," said the doctor with a little reservation in his voice.

"What do you think it is, doc?" Arnold asked.

"I won't know until we get the test results, but I can assure you I'll be on this with all the urgency I can. When I get the outcomes, my office will call you for another appointment. It will probably be the day after tomorrow."

"Is that it?" Arnold asked.

"Mr. Glassman, I can't see inside you. I'll have this sample analyzed. I'll get you set up for the MRI and the blood test. Until I get the results, we'll have to wait."

Arnold was not very good at waiting.

"Okay, doc. Thank you. Let me know when and where to go for the tests."

Arnold looked at his watch. 4:30 p.m. For the first time he could remember, he had no thoughts. He didn't know what to do or what to say.

Then it hit him. He was having dinner with Kacie at six. What would he say to her? Should he tell her about the doctor's appointment and the tests? He decided to keep this all to himself for the time being. He'd wait for the results before he'd say anything to anybody.

Arnold stared blankly at the certificates on the wall as he buttoned his shirt, pondering the worst that could happen. He went to the desk to check out and get the directions for his tests, and then he went back to the office.

* * *

Just outside the medical building, Harold Longwood appeared out of nowhere. Just *poof* and there he was.

"Wow!" he said as he looked around. "They sure move fast in heaven!"

"Harold, the man you're going to help will be coming out of the building right behind you in a couple of minutes."

"Peter, is that you?" Harold asked as he looked around.

"Who else would it be? I told you that you'd be able to hear my voice, didn't I?"

"That's right, sorry."

"No need to apologize, Harold. Keep your eyes on that door. When Arnold comes out—"

"Arnold, that's the guy I'll be helping," Harold repeated.

"Yes, his name is Arnold. When he comes out, I want you to walk with him to his car and tell him that everything will be okay."

"You're kidding." said Harold with reservation in his voice.

"No, I'm not kidding."

"I'm not going to tell him I'm an angel or the fact that no one else can see me or—"

"Harold, you've got to get a grip. This is not *It's a Wonderful Life* or any other movie you've seen. Just do what I tell you to do."

"Okay, Peter. Whatever you say."

A moment later Arnold emerged from the building with a very somber look on his face. He glanced around, trying to remember where he'd parked his car. He walked toward the parking lot.

"That's him, Harold. Remember, just tell him everything will be okay," said Peter. "And, Harold, try to be reassuring. Don't creep him out."

"Right," Harold said sarcastically as he walked up alongside Arnold. "Hey, Arnold, how're you doing?"

The businessman turned and stopped, puzzled as someone he didn't recall spoke to him. "How do you know my name? Do I know you?"

Harold stood there and looked up expectantly. "Well?" he said.

"Well what?" said Arnold.

"Not you, Arnold. I'm waiting for Peter to tell me what I'm supposed to say."

"This is crazy," Arnold said as he started toward his car.

"I'm not crazy, just waiting for my instructions."

"What instructions?" said Arnold, more agitated now.

"Wait a minute! I've already got my instructions. I'm supposed to tell you that everything is going to be okay. That's it! Arnold, you're going to be okay. Have you got that?"

As soon as he'd said those words, Harold disappeared. Right before Arnold's eyes. *Poof.* He was gone. Arnold's mouth opened. He rubbed his eyes and looked around, searching for the crazy man who'd just told him everything was going to be okay. But Harold was nowhere to be seen.

Other pedestrians paused to stare at Arnold as he spoke to himself and looked all around. When the businessman noticed all the attention, he quickly moved to his car and drove away.

He looked in the rearview mirror and took a deep breath.

"So I guess I'm going crazy along with being terminal. That's all I need! Who in blazes was that nut?"

Even though he was agitated by Harold's appearance and pronouncement, Arnold was certainly intrigued with the crazy man's comment that everything was going to be okay.

Arnold was bombarded with questions by a couple of managers as soon as he returned to the office, but he didn't notice them as he shut his office door. The two executives looked at each other, shrugged their shoulders, and left.

Mrs. DeBarry knocked on the door, but Arnold didn't respond. She knocked louder and opened it.

"Yes, Mrs. DeBarry, what is it?"

"Mr. Glassman, are you okay?"

"What?" he said sharply.

"I asked if you were okay?"

"Yes, yes, I'm fine. Please shut the door."

Mrs. DeBarry had been his administrative assistant for twenty-five years. She knew him better than anyone, apart from his daughter. She knew he wasn't being honest. But she closed the door and did as he said.

Arnold leaned back in his chair and stared at the ceiling. Again, he began to cough and wheeze.

Poof. Harold appeared out of nowhere. Arnold almost fell out of his chair.

"How the devil did you get in here? You're that crazy man from outside my doctor's office. What kind of nut are you? How did you get in here!"

Harold was a little surprised himself as he looked around.

"Sorry, Arnold. I have no control over when they do something like this," he said with a bit of a chuckle.

"They? Who are they? How do you know my name? How did you get in here? Who in the world are you?" Arnold asked, each question louder than the last.

Harold stood there, looking up, waiting for Peter's help. But nothing came.

"I'm waiting for Peter to tell me what to say, but I guess he wants me to reaffirm what I said earlier. Everything is going to be okay!"

"What's going to be okay?" said Arnold, coughing after each word.

"Hey, that's a bad cough. You better see a doctor about that."

"I just came from the doctor, you idiot!" said Arnold.

"That's right, you did. Maybe that's why he wanted me to say everything would be okay. Did you get some bad news?"

"My news is none of your business! Who wanted you to say everything would be okay?" said Arnold in a calmer tone than before.

"Peter!" said Harold with a smile.

"Saint Peter?" said Arnold with a look of amazement.

"That's right! But I'm on a first-name basis with him. I mean, he told me to call him Peter," Harold said, sticking out his chest.

Arnold sat back in his chair, closed his eyes, and rubbed his face. He looked back at Harold again. "Maybe I'm the one who's going crazy."

"You're not going crazy, Arnold."

"Who are you?" said Arnold, a little more at ease.

"Harold Longwood. Firefighter and paramedic. I was going to say Harold Longwood, AS2, but that's because I'm such a fan of *It's a Wonderful Life*."

Arnold sat there with his mouth open. He had no idea what the man meant.

"You know. Angel, second-class?" said Harold.

"Angel?" Arnold said a little more nervously.

"Well, I really don't know how this stuff works, but I'm supposed to be a helper to you. And so far the only thing I've been told to do is to tell you that everything is going to be okay."

And as soon as he said that, Harold disappeared again.

Arnold couldn't believe it. A man had disappeared in front of him *twice* today. Maybe he really was going crazy.

Suddenly, Mrs. DeBarry entered the office. "Mr. Glassman, I heard you talking, almost shouting, and I didn't see a light on your phone. Was someone in your office? How did they get past me? Are you okay?"

"Yes, I'm okay. It was nothing. I was just talking to myself." Then he added, "Talking to myself rather loudly, I fear."

"Yes sir. If you need anything, Mr. Glassman, I hope you'll let me help."

"Thank you, Mrs. DeBarry. I'll call on you if I do."

He looked at his watch. 5:30 p.m. He better go to the restaurant to meet Kacie.

As Arnold left the office, a number of managers began to pepper him with questions. Again, Arnold didn't answer as he entered the elevator.

He stood alone in the elevator. "Angel, second-class!"

CHAPTER SIX
My Baby Girl

Arnold was sitting at the table, staring out the window, when he heard Kacie's voice.

"Hi, Daddy!"

He stood, gave her a big hug, kissed her cheek, and then pulled a chair out for her.

"Thanks so much for taking the time to meet me for dinner, Daddy!" Kacie said as she unfolded her napkin.

"I'd rather spend time with my baby girl than anyone else in the world, including the president of the United States!" Arnold said smiling.

"Wow! That's saying a lot since I know how much you like him," Kacie said and chuckled.

"Well, I don't want to talk about him. How in the world are you doing, sweetheart?"

"I'm doing fine. I'm really having a great year. I've got some wonderful kids."

"I can't imagine having that many kids around me all day. I don't know how you do it, honey. I'd go stark raving mad."

"I love kids, Daddy."

"Well, if I'm ever going to be a grandfather, you'd better find the right man. I'm not going to live forever, you know."

"Oh, Daddy. They will have to run you down on Judgment Day and catch you."

Arnold suddenly coughed and began wheezing. He covered his mouth with his napkin and coughed more.

Kacie looked concerned.

After a minute, Arnold stopped coughing. He crunched the napkin in his hand and hid it under the table.

"Daddy, that's a terrible cough. Are you all right?"

"I'm fine. I think I'm getting a cold or something. I'll call my doctor and get him to phone a prescription in for me. I'll take care of it tomorrow. Don't you worry yourself about your old dad."

"I do worry about you, Daddy. You don't take care of yourself, and you certainly don't eat the way you should."

"I'll be okay, honey."

"Well, maybe you should make an appointment and get your doctor to check you out."

"Nonsense, I'll be okay."

As the server walked up to take their orders, Arnold looked under the table to see if anything was in the napkin.

The same bloody-looking mass as before. He crunched the napkin up and placed it on his chair to hide it from Kacie.

Before the server left, Arnold requested another napkin.

"So, Daddy, what's going on at the company?"

"Well, there's been a lot of changes in the industry over the last few years. I should have made some adjustments a long time ago, but I didn't. Still, I've got some good people who are working to right the ship. Everything will be okay. Right now, things are a little shaky, but we'll be okay. For the time being, we need to make some cutbacks and temporarily lay off some people."

"That's terrible, especially with the holidays coming up. Those poor people," Kacie said with remorse.

"Well, we're only getting rid of the ones who aren't important."

"Daddy! I can't believe you said that. You've always considered all of your employees to be important."

"Well . . . you know what I mean!" said Arnold, trying to cover up for his harshness.

"I guess I do. I've just never heard you say something like that."

"I'm sorry, honey. I guess I've had a lot on my mind. Maybe I'm not feeling as benevolent as I should."

"What's on your mind, Dad? You can talk to me."

With that, Arnold started to share his concerns about who would eventually take over for him and run the company. After a while, Kacie looked down because she felt guilty that she wasn't going to fulfill his wishes to take over the company when the time came.

"Don't you worry about that, young lady. I'm very happy my daughter is a teacher. She's the best tea—"

Suddenly Arnold was racked with another coughing spell. He picked up the napkin from his chair and coughed into it. Even other people sitting nearby looked on in concern.

"Daddy, I want you to call your doctor immediately! You need to see him as soon as possible. That's a terrible cough."

"Okay, honey, I'll call first thing in the morning. His office is already closed for the day."

"Promise me?"

"Yes, sweetheart. I'll make the call."

Their food arrived, and for the rest of their time together, Arnold had occasional coughing spells. When they finished the meal, he hugged Kacie as they were leaving. Near the door, when she wasn't looking, he put his napkin in the trash.

Outside, Kacie took his arm.

"Daddy, I love you so much. I'm concerned about your coughing. I hope your doctor takes care of it for you."

"Oh, honey, I'm sure he will."

"Daddy, I pray for you every day."

"Thanks, baby. I know you do, and it means so much to me. I'll be okay. An angel told me so today."

"Really? I've never heard you say anything like that before. I'm just glad you were listening."

They chatted as he walked her to her car. The last thing she said was, "Bye, Daddy. I love you!"

"Bye, baby. I love you too," he said and hugged her.

Arnold walked to his car. He felt as if he were carrying the weight of the world on his shoulders. When he sat in the driver's seat, he leaned his head on the headrest.

"Dear God," he prayed. "I sure haven't been the kind of man I should have been. I'm scared now, God. I don't know what to do. I've got a feeling the news isn't going to be good. Who'll take over my company? Who'll take care of my baby girl?"

He began to cry as he leaned forward, put his hands on the steering wheel, and rested his head on his hands.

* * *

Harold watched the scene as if it were a movie. He looked at Peter and said, "Are you sure everything is going to be okay?"

"Yes, Harold. I told you it would be and it will be. You're a big part of the solution to everything Arnold is going through. You'll understand more as things play out."

"I wish I had your confidence," Harold said as he shook his head.

CHAPTER SEVEN
You're Fired!

Bret walked into his cubicle, booted up his computer, and sat down. He took a deep breath and closed his eyes for a moment. He had been through a lot in the last twenty-four hours. His dad's funeral and Angie breaking up with him. But he felt positive about his life as a whole. He'd rebound from this, pick up the pieces. He still had his job, and he really enjoyed what he was doing.

"Hey, Bret. I'm so sorry to hear about your dad!" said Ed Harper from an adjoining cubicle.

"Thanks, Ed."

"Is your mom still around?"

"No. She died in an automobile accident years ago," Bret said somberly.

"Any brothers or sisters?"

"No, just me now."

"Well, I'm so sorry."

"Thanks, Ed," Bret said as he tidied his desk, moving some things around.

"By the way," Ed said, "something's going on. Several people have received notes to meet with McCarty. At least it's not with HR. So that's a good thing, right?"

Bret's eyes fell on an envelope with his name on it. The message inside said he was to meet with the CFO at 9:30.

"What in the world?" said Bret as he sat back in his chair.

Bret had begun working at Glassman Industries right out of college. But he had never advanced from his position in the five years he worked for the company. Bret didn't understand why he hadn't moved up the ranks. He had graduated at the top of his class, and he had a degree or two more than the people who'd been promoted over him.

But he wasn't the most outgoing person. He never tooted his own horn. He had gone to his boss a couple of times and suggested ways the company could increase profits in several areas, but that was always the end of it. He never received any kind of response. And over time, those suggestions were implemented, so he figured someone else had had the same ideas.

What he didn't know was that his boss had presented Bret's ideas as his own. As a result, he had moved up the ranks, and Bret had found he had a new boss. Eventually, Bret learned what his manager had done, and so he stopped making suggestions. What was the use if someone was going to take credit for his ideas?

Bret accomplished a couple of tasks before his appointment with McCarty. As he walked to the CFO's office, he tried to figure out what was going on. Maybe his old boss had come clean about how he'd exploited Bret's ideas. No, he'd never do that. Well, he'd find out soon.

Bret knocked on the door and entered. Personally, he didn't like McCarty. He struck Bret as a snob. McCarty wasn't that much older than Bret, and they'd had about the same education. But McCarty was someone who did toot his own horn.

When Bret walked in, the CFO didn't look up from his desk. He was buried in whatever he was reading and occasionally sipped his coffee. Bret sat in the chair in front of McCarty's desk and waited to hear whatever this meeting was going to be about.

With no chitchat or "How are things going, Bret?" or "Sorry to hear about your dad," the CFO stoically turned Bret's world upside down.

"Bret, I'm sorry to have to tell you, but we're having to make some difficult cutbacks and we need to let some people go. Unfortunately, you're one of those people."

"What?" Bret said, surprised and stunned.

"You'll need to clean out your things as soon as possible. You'll receive two weeks' pay in addition to any unused vacation and sick time you've accumulated—"

"Why? What did I do?"

"You haven't done anything. There have been a lot of changes in the business, and we need to adjust, which means the company has to make some very difficult decisions. Unfortunately, you're one of the people affected by this decision. Your position isn't essential, and we can cover your job with other people."

Bret couldn't believe it. Normally, he was shy and quiet. But after two major blows to his life the last week or so, he responded like never before. "I've given everything to this company. I've never missed a day of work—until yesterday. My job is not important?"

"Well, maybe you shouldn't have missed yesterday," McCarty said with a snobby sneer.

"I missed a *day* to attend my father's *funeral*. I believe the employee handbook classifies that as *compassionate* leave." Bret hoped his emphasized words would hit home.

"Oh, er, I'm sorry to hear about your loss. But that doesn't change anything. You need to clean out your desk as soon as you leave this office. Security will escort you from the property," McCarty said with no hint of sympathy in his voice.

"Escorted out by security?" Bret said with a flabbergasted look.

"Yes. It's company policy."

"Mr. McCarty, I've never said anything about this before, but you know those two adjustments we made last year with the shipping procedures?"

"Yes," McCarty said with a smile, looking Bret in the eyes. "I do. They saved the company a great deal of money. Dan Becton did a great job with those recommendations." McCarty returned to his papers and silently dismissed Bret from his office.

"Well, those weren't Mr. Becton's ideas. They were *my* suggestions."

McCarty put down the papers. "Bret, I don't think it's a good idea to make up stories at a time like this to try to save your job."

"I'm not making this up. Those were *my* proposals. I talked them over with Mr. Becton, and he told me he'd get back to me. But instead, he took my ideas and presented them as his own. I never said anything because I thought that was the right thing to do—be a team player," Bret said, his voice rising with every sentence.

"The decision has been made, Bret," McCarty ended the conversation. "Again, I'm sorry. You're dismissed."

Bret sat for a moment and stared at the CFO. But McCarty never looked back at Bret, focusing his attention on the papers on his desk and his coffee. He showed no remorse at all to someone he had just fired. Finally, Bret got up and walked out of the office.

He walked slowly back to his desk. He was in a fog. His dad had died. Angie had broken their engagement. And now he'd lost his job. He had never felt more distraught in his life. He suddenly had nothing. Absolutely nothing. Less than nothing!

Bret returned to his cubicle and collapsed in his chair. He took a deep breath and closed his eyes. When he opened them again, he noticed some coworkers hovering around him. Ed stood at the entrance to his cubicle.

"Hey, Bret, they're not letting you go, are they?" Ed asked. "Tom, George, and Naymond have already cleaned out their cubes. Why are they getting rid of all the good people?"

"McCarty fired me too."

"No way! You're one of the best employees this company has. Why'd they fire you?"

"I guess it was just a numbers game and my number came up. McCarty said my job wasn't important," Bret said and opened his desk drawer.

"I'm sorry, man. I wish I could do something."

"Thanks, Ed. But I guess I'm in a giant toilet and someone is getting ready to flush it. What in the world is going on? God, is there anything else You can do to make my life more miserable than it is now?" he said, almost shouting as he looked up. As if in answer to his question, Angie's picture fell off the wall and hit the floor with a loud bang.

Bret rolled his eyes and looked upward again, shaking his head.

Coworkers in other nearby cubicles craned their heads to see what was going on as Bret ranted. When he looked toward them, they all ducked back down.

Bret burned inside as he thought about Arnold Glassman allowing him to be fired. He thought about how faithful he had been, how he'd never done anything in any of the gray areas that might compromise his position with the company. And after five years of devoted service, he was being let go and even told that his position wasn't that important.

Bret noticed some people putting up a Christmas tree and beginning to decorate it. In a little over two weeks, it would be Christmas. And he would be going through Christmas without any family, without Angie, and without a job.

"Ho, Ho, Ho, Merry Christmas!" Bret murmured under his breath.

Soon one of the security officers showed up at Bret's cubicle with a couple of boxes.

"Mr. Davidson, I'm Joe Thomas with security. I'm here to help you with your things."

Bret rolled his eyes and emptied the contents of his desk. One of the last things he picked up was Angie's photograph. He looked at it for a moment and then put it in the trash.

As Bret was escorted down the hallway, he felt like a dead man walking. People looked up from their desks as he passed, but others only looked after he had passed.

When he exited the building, Joe laid the box he was carrying on the sidewalk and turned to walk back inside. He didn't say a word. No "Sorry for your luck!" or sorry about anything. He didn't even offer to help him to his car.

Bret put his box on top of the other one and balanced both as he walked to his car. He placed the boxes in the back seat. When he sat down in the driver's seat, he looked in the rearview mirror and began to seethe with anger. He started the car and pulled out of the parking garage. As he made his way to the exit, he glanced at the best parking space available. It said "Reserved, Arnold Glassman."

Bret stopped the car and looked over at the parking space and said, "One day, one day, Mr. Glassman, you'll get yours."

Chapter Eight

Fill Me In!

In heaven, Harold was looking around. "Wow! Things sure move quickly around here!"

"Harold?"

"Yes, Saint Peter, er, Mr. Peter."

"Peter will do."

"I'm sorry. I was just trying to be polite," Harold said.

"I know, Harold. It's okay."

"I did what you told me to do. I told him everything would be okay. What'll we do now?"

"I know you did, Harold. I thought it might help you to know a little bit about Arnold Glassman. But it doesn't look right for one of our ambassadors to be looking up and asking for instructions. You make people nervous when you do things like that."

Harold looked down and squinted as he listened to Peter. Had he done something wrong? "But no one but Arnold can see me, right?" Harold asked.

"Yes, that's true. But we don't want Arnold to look like a lunatic every time you show up."

"I did the best I could, Peter."

"I know you did, Harold. I'm just trying to help you so you won't be so unsure of yourself."

"You know, I prided myself on knowing my work when I was a firefighter. We trained for every possibility. We were prepared for the worst. I was a really good firefighter."

"I know you were, and you'll be a great ambassador for heaven to Arnold Glassman."

"You know, Arnold seems impatient and very distraught," Harold said.

"He received some pretty disturbing news today. He has been coughing up blood and wheezing. The doctor wasn't very reassuring with his exam today. So Arnold fears the worst."

"Is it cancer?" Harold asked.

"Well, let's just say what I told you to say to him: everything is going to be okay. Arnold's wife left him a long time ago. And he raised his daughter alone."

"He has no family other than his daughter?" questioned Harold.

"That's right. Arnold always hoped his daughter would take over the company one day, but Kacie turned out to be a teacher. There's no one else on his management team that he trusts to take over the company."

"Kacie isn't married then?"

"No. She doesn't even have a boyfriend."

"Is she ugly?"

"That's a terrible question!"

"I'm sorry, but it was an honest question. I was just thinking maybe she's a troll and that's why she's never found anyone."

"To the contrary, she's a very beautiful woman." Immediately an image appeared of Kacie so Harold could see for himself.

"Wow! She's a looker!"

"Harold!"

"I don't mean any disrespect. It's just a common term these days for good-looking women. It's hard to believe a young lady like that doesn't have a couple of guys hanging around, waiting for her to throw out the dishwater."

Peter gave him a very quizzical look and mouthed the word *dishwater*.

"Harold, over the years, several young men attempted to get her attention. But she wanted to finish school and settle in as a teacher. And she has very high moral standards and wasn't going to settle for just anyone."

"You don't find a lot of young people like that anymore," said Harold.

"You're exactly right. Arnold has a wonderful daughter."

"What else do I need to know about Arnold?"

"Excellent question, Harold! You need to know that very soon Arnold will attempt to do something very bad.

You will be there to stop him. It will also be up to you to decide how you will stop him."

"What's he going to do?"

"I brought you here to fill you in with what you need to know, not tell you everything. You'll know what to do at the time, and you'll make the right decision to help Arnold."

"May I ask a question? Well, it's not really a question. It's more like a request."

"What is it?"

"You know, Peter, it would be a lot easier for me down there if I could fly."

Peter shook his head. "Harold, I think we've talked quite enough for the moment. I think it would be good for you to look at what's taking place at Arnold's company. Maybe that will help you as you plan to help Arnold."

"You mean I can see what's been going on with Arnold's company?" Harold asked with wide eyes.

"Yes. I'll have Matthew show you how you can access that information."

A young man dressed like Peter smiled and put a hand on Harold's shoulder.

"Take a seat, Harold, and I'll show you how to see what's been going on," Matthew said as he pulled out a chair for Harold.

"Arnold has been listening to his chief financial officer, William McCarty, about making cuts to the company's workforce."

Harold watched as Matthew showed him a procession of people being let go by the CFO. Harold was especially taken with Bret Davidson. He wanted to know more about him and what had been going on in his life.

Matthew told him about the passing of Bret's dad, Angie's breaking up with him, and his meeting with McCarty.

"Bret doesn't have another job yet?"

"No, he was just fired."

"And he doesn't have another girlfriend?"

"No, Angie just broke up with him the night before."

Harold looked at the picture of Bret and said, "That young man needs as much help as Arnold." He smiled and closed his eyes as if some things had finally added up in his uncertain mind. "Matthew, can you get a message to Peter?" Harold asked.

"Sure," he said.

"Can he arrange it so another person, besides Arnold Glassman, can see me?"

Matthew had an "aha" look and asked, "Bret Davidson?"

"Exactly!" said Harold.

"I think we can arrange that for you. I'm sure Peter would agree to that request. I'll take care of it as soon as we finish."

CHAPTER NINE
Boy Meets Girl

Harold was waiting outside Bret's home, ready to strike up a conversation when Bret came out to pick up his paper. Even though Harold didn't have a lot of confidence in what he was doing, he was beginning to enjoy this work.

Bret Davidson was one of the most organized people anyone ever knew. He had schedules for everything. He always did his laundry on Thursday evenings while watching his favorite TV show. He always washed his car and mowed the lawn on Saturdays. He paid his bills on Monday evenings. He worked out every other day. He made the next day's lunch every evening, right before he went to bed. And he always set his alarm just before he turned in.

But for the first time in years, Bret didn't set his alarm.

This morning was different. At least, that was the plan. He was going to sleep until he woke up naturally. When he did, he glanced at the clock. But things hadn't really changed that much, because he woke up at the same time his alarm usually went off.

He closed his eyes and tried to go back to sleep, but it didn't work. So he got up and got dressed, following his normal routine. After all, he was a creature of habit.

Bret walked outside to get his newspaper and noticed Harold on the sidewalk, looking around.

"May I help you?" Bret said as he bent over to pick up his paper.

"No, I was just out for a walk. I was enjoying the cool air. How are you doing this beautiful morning?"

"Oh, I've been better. But I'm sure I'll make it," Bret said with a little hesitancy.

"Oh, I'm sorry. My name is Harold. You're Bret Davidson, right?"

"How did you know that?" Bret said with suspicion in his voice.

Harold felt a little nervous but said with a chuckle, "Your name is on the mailbox."

"Oh, yeah. Sorry for my tone."

"No need. Bret, you seem to have a lot on your mind."

"How would you know that? You don't even know me."

"Oh, I'm a good judge of character and emotions. You know, it might be a good idea to talk with your pastor.

Maybe he could help you. Oh, well, I must be going. Have a nice day, Bret."

As Harold walked away briskly, Bret stared at the strange man and wondered about their peculiar conversation.

He looked through the paper as he ate breakfast. At least he could check out the classified section and see what kinds of jobs were available. After all, he had a couple of degrees, he was smart, and he was dependable. Surely someone needed someone like him. He wrote down some possibilities and addresses on the list he had made from his online searches the night before. After cleaning up, he sat down for a moment to collect his thoughts before going out the door.

On the end table, he saw Pastor McDowell's card. That's strange, he thought. "If there is ever anything I can do to be of help, please don't hesitate to call on me. And Bret, I really mean that." Maybe the strange guy out front this morning was right. Perhaps the pastor might be able to give Bret some encouragement, some advice. Bret picked up his cell and called.

Almost immediately the pastor answered.

"Pastor McDowell. May I help you?"

"Yes, Pastor. This is Bret Davidson."

"Hello, Bret. I was just thinking about you. How are you doing?"

"Well, I was wondering if you might have a few minutes this morning to talk. I know it's spur of the moment, and if you're busy, I sure understand."

"I'd be more than happy to talk, Bret. Do you know the coffee shop at the corner of Main and First?"

"I do. That's not far from where I live."

"That was your dad's favorite place to meet. How about I meet you there in twenty minutes?"

"Great! I'll see you there."

Bret hung up and closed his eyes. He was second-guessing himself about calling Pastor McDowell. He even thought about calling back and canceling. But as he looked at his cell phone, he shook his head and headed out the door.

Bret parked at the coffee shop and started to open his door. In the next car, he saw a pretty girl with her head down, eyes closed, and lips moving. He couldn't help but stare. She was beautiful.

"Wow," he thought, "I just got ditched by Angie, and here I am staring at another girl."

They both got out of their cars at the same time, and Bret decided to say something.

"Don't worry. The coffee's not that bad here."

"Excuse me?" Kacie Glassman said.

"You looked a little hesitant about going inside. I'm just saying the coffee's not that bad."

"Oh, I was praying," Kacie said as she smiled.

"That's interesting. I'm here to meet a pastor for coffee, and the first thing I see when I get here is a beautiful woman praying," Bret said with a smile.

"Well, enjoy your time and your coffee."

"Thanks," he answered. Bret even had the opportunity to open the door for Kacie.

As soon as he walked in, he saw Pastor McDowell at a corner table with two cups of coffee.

Kacie also saw Pastor McDowell. She smiled and waved, and the pastor waved back.

But Bret thought he was waving at him.

"I hope you take your coffee with cream and two sugars," said Pastor McDowell.

"That's fine, Pastor. Thanks so much for meeting me."

"I'm glad you called me, Bret."

Bret saw Kacie sitting alone with her coffee as he began the conversation with the pastor.

"Well, Pastor, I've had a couple of other tragedies since my father passed away last week."

"I'm sorry to hear that. What's happened?"

"Well, after the funeral, my fiancée broke up with me. And yesterday, I was fired."

"Oh, Bret! I'm so sorry."

"Angie, my fiancée, said I wasn't going places like she wanted to go, and my boss said the company didn't think I was important enough to keep. Pastor, do you think God is mad at me?"

"Bret, tragedy doesn't happen because God's mad at us."

"Well, He must be awfully mad at me. My world has completely crashed in on me."

"I believe sometimes God allows things to happen to get our attention. Sometimes, He allows things to happen because He has something greater for us. I hope that's the case for you, Bret. Maybe He's doing both: getting your attention and getting you to a greater future."

"Oh, I don't know, Pastor. I haven't given God much time lately. My dad really liked you and the church. He tried to get me to go with him a couple of times."

Bret looked down at the table.

"Bret, every journey starts with the first step. Why don't you come this Sunday? If, after the service, you don't feel it's for you, I can suggest some other churches in the area. Surely there's one around here that can minister to you."

Bret glanced toward Kacie again. She must have sensed it because she turned and made eye contact with him.

Bret quickly turned back to Pastor McDowell. Kacie smiled at catching him.

"I never thought about things like that. Maybe God is trying to get my attention and maybe He does have something better for me."

"Christmas is around the corner, Bret. It's a time that reminds us of God's greatest gift to us. I hope you'll come this Sunday."

As Bret was about to answer, he noticed Kacie was getting up to leave. He quickly said a thank you and told the pastor he would think about it. Right now, he really wanted to talk with her before she disappeared.

Bret shook the pastor's hand and headed out the door. As he was walking out, Kacie was getting into her car.

"I hope your coffee wasn't as strong as mine was. I probably won't sleep much tonight." Bret said raising his cup in a kind of salute.

"Caffeine doesn't affect me like that. But mine was good."

"My name is Bret," he said as he walked toward her.

"My name is Kacie. Kacie Glassman," she said as she smiled.

Almost immediately, Bret said, "If I never hear that name again in my life, it will be too soon!" Almost as quickly, he couldn't believe he'd said that out loud.

"Excuse me!" Kacie said indignantly.

"I'm sorry. There's no way someone as beautiful as you could be related to a total creep like Arnold Glassman."

"Arnold Glassman is my *father*!" Kacie said as she got into her car and slammed the door.

Bret watched her drive off. "And the hits just keep on coming!" he mumbled to himself

Harold stood outside the coffee shop, watching Bret sit in his car. He shook his head. "I sure hope you know what you're doing, Peter. Maybe it wasn't such a good idea giving me this job. My first plan looks like a total flop. Maybe I made a mistake."

"Give it time, Harold. I think it's a great plan," Peter said.

Chapter Ten
Arnold's Bad News

Arnold started his day as he always did—coffee first. He turned the machine on and walked out to get his paper. He always read the paper with his first cup of coffee. He noticed the air was colder. Too cold for him to take his time outside, strolling the sidewalk a couple of times to get his system churning a bit.

When he walked back into the house, the smell of coffee delighted his senses. As he laid his paper on the table, he put some instant oatmeal in the microwave and then poured a cup of coffee.

He began to lightly wheeze, then his breathing became labored, and finally he broke into a coughing spasm. He went to the counter and grabbed a paper towel. As he coughed into it, he saw the familiar bloody mass. He closed his eyes and grimaced as he threw the paper towel into the trash.

When he sat at the table with his oatmeal and coffee, he opened the paper and scanned the front page. The headline predicted it was going to be a poor Christmas financially for local businesses.

"Well, it's not just *my* business that's being affected," he said out loud.

Arnold continued to read the paper as he finished his coffee and oatmeal. Then he had another coughing spell. When he discarded another paper towel, he heard the phone ring.

"Arnold Glassman," he answered with authority.

"Mr. Glassman, this is Dr. Martin's office. The doctor would like to see if you could come in this afternoon at two o'clock."

"Yes, I'll be there," Arnold said reluctantly.

"Fine. I'll let Dr. Martin know. Have a nice day!" the nurse said cheerfully.

"That's easy for you to say," Arnold thought. He also thought the news couldn't be good if the doctor wanted to see him this quickly.

Arnold dressed and went to the office. Maybe he wouldn't think about it if he just followed his routine. People spoke to him as he walked to his office, but he didn't hear them. They were still talking and asking questions when he closed the door behind him.

He sat in his chair, leaned back, and closed his eyes. He didn't feel like working. He buzzed Mrs. DeBarry and asked her to come in.

She brought her legal pad and pen and sat down in front of his desk, as she normally did, ready to take notes for whatever Arnold wanted her to do. After all, she had been with him for years, and by now, she knew him pretty well.

"No need for the pad. I just want to talk . . . if that's okay with you," he said quietly.

"Oh my, are you letting me go, Mr. Glassman?" she asked, tearing up.

"No, no. Of course not! What in the world would give you that idea?"

"Well, others are being let go, and I feared maybe you were firing me rather than let Mr. McCarty do it."

"Mrs. DeBarry, you've been with me longer than anyone else in this company. You've seen the company grow. No one knows me better than you. How in heaven's name could you ever think I would let you go?"

"I'm sorry. I guess I'm just a little on edge. To be honest, Mr. Glassman, you haven't been yourself lately. You've never acted the way you've been acting lately. I really don't know what to think."

"I know and I'm sorry about that. That's why I asked you to come in. I just need to talk with someone. You see, I'm not well."

Before Arnold could go any further, Mrs. DeBarry interrupted him. "What's wrong, Mr. Glassman?"

"I've got a doctor's appointment at two this afternoon, and hopefully I'll find out what's wrong. But frankly, I fear the worst."

"I'm sure you'll be okay, Mr. Glassman. You've always been so healthy. I can't remember the last time you were ill."

"Well, I've been thinking about what I would do if the news is as devastating as I believe it will be. I'm a successful businessman, but I don't have a will. Of course, I want everything to go to my daughter."

Arnold began to tear up. "How will she get along without me? She doesn't have anyone but me. She'll be devastated to hear the news."

"Mr. Glassman, you're talking like you already know the news will be bad. Let's wait until you see the doctor. Perhaps you're worrying about nothing."

"That's why I wanted to talk to you, young lady. You've always lifted my spirits when things were down. You're a wonderful person, Mrs. DeBarry. You're a great employee. No, you're more like family than anyone else in my company."

"Thank you, sir. You've always been so good to me. I've always wanted to do my best for you."

"And you have always done a great job . . . I'll . . . I'll . . . make sure . . . you're taken care of if the news is as bad as I think it will be."

"Mr. Glassman, please don't talk like that."

"You're right. Thank you so much for cheering me up. You can go back to your office now."

"Please call me after your appointment, and let me know how you are."

"I will. I will. Thank you again."

Time passed slowly for Arnold until it was time for his appointment. Then it seemed to rush ahead. He made his way to the doctor's office.

"Hello, Mr. Glassman. The doctor will see you in just a moment. Please follow me," the nurse said and then led him into the doctor's office.

Arnold had never been in this office before. This seemed to be another indication the news was bad.

Dr. Martin walked in and took a seat at his desk. "Mr. Glassman, the news isn't good, I'm sorry to say," he said reluctantly. "You have cancer, Mr. Glassman. And unfortunately, it's a very aggressive cancer. The prognosis is not good."

"How long do I have, doc?" Arnold said, looking down.

"I'm not a hundred percent sure, but probably four to six weeks. I'd like to recommend Dr. Fusselle, an oncologist, to develop a treatment plan. We could try some treatments, but I don't think it will help you with your quality of life during such a short time. Mr. Glassman, as things progress, you're going to experience great pain, and it won't be easy for your family as they watch you deteriorate. I recommend going into hospice when the time comes. I want to be absolutely honest with you about the prognosis. I'm so sorry to share this news with you. If

I can do anything to help, please do not hesitate to call on me."

"Thank you, doctor. I appreciate your candor."

Arnold left the office but paused in the hall in a kind of daze. Then he remembered the peculiar man who approached him after his last appointment. He began looking around to see if the odd man was somewhere around. When he didn't see him, he walked to his car.

As he sat in his car, he wondered who he should call. He certainly didn't want to call Kacie just yet, and he really didn't feel like calling Mrs. DeBarry. He decided to go home and ponder his plans. He had a great many things to get in order.

When Arnold entered his house, he walked straight to his bedroom and took off his coat and tie. He wanted to change into something more comfortable and then think about his options.

He opened a dresser drawer and saw a handgun. Arnold stared at it and grimaced and slowly closed the drawer.

CHAPTER ELEVEN
Give Me a Second Chance

Bret sat at the dining room table and went through that morning's classified ads. He added another possibility to the list of places he planned to apply for employment, both online and in person. His confidence was low as he closed the paper and placed the list in his shirt pocket.

He put on his coat and headed out the door. He knew the holiday season was not the best time to be looking for something permanent. But he had to try.

As he walked out of his house, he saw Harold walking by. "Nice day for a cup of coffee, huh, Bret?"

Bret's face had a perplexed look as he watched the strange man. "I wonder if he lives in the neighborhood. We're getting some strange people in my neck of the woods," he said as he got into his car.

But then he thought, before going out into the cruel world, maybe it would be good to get a cup of coffee. His mind, though, was still on his unemployment. The economy was terrible, and he probably wouldn't be able to find anything until after Christmas.

He decided to walk to Starbucks. After waiting in line, placing his order, and paying his bill, he turned around and saw Kacie Glassman at a table. She was sipping her coffee and reading her Bible. He swallowed hard and walked over to her table.

"I know you probably don't want to hear anything I have to say, but I'd like to explain my rudeness the other day."

"There's no need. Thank you anyway!" Kacie said curtly, without looking up.

"I see you're reading the Bible. Do you think there's anything in there about giving me another chance?" he said reverently.

He was shocked when she smiled and looked up at him.

"Touché, Bret. That was a very clever response. Okay, sit down."

"You remembered my name."

"You did tell me your name the last time. So what do you have to explain about our last conversation?"

"Uh, yeah . . . uh, I worked for your dad's company for five years. And to be honest, it was the only anchor in my life after two recent tragedies."

"I'm sorry to hear that."

"Thank you. They were pretty bad. You see, my father passed away unexpectedly."

"Oh, Bret, I'm so sorry."

"Thank you. He was a great guy."

"And then, surprisingly, my fiancée ended our engagement the night of my dad's funeral."

Kacie shook her head and looked down.

Bret continued, "But at least I still had my job. Or so I thought."

"My dad fired you?" Kacie said with a look of horror.

"Well, it wasn't actually him. It was the CFO—that jackal, Bill McCarty."

"To be honest with you, I've never been very fond of Mr. McCarty either. I think he's forced my dad to make some bad decisions."

"Well, being told that your job isn't important anymore certainly doesn't help your self-esteem."

"Oh, Bret, I'm so sorry. I'm going to talk with my dad and see about getting your job back."

"No, please don't do that. I'll manage. I had some good ideas and even had a couple of them put into action that saved the company a lot of money. Unfortunately, my supervisor presented my ideas as his own, and there was nothing I could do about it. But that's behind me now. I'm a smart, hardworking man, and I'll land on my feet."

"Well, I wish you'd let me to talk to my dad."

"Thank you, but no, please don't. To be honest, after the way our last conversation ended, I'm just thrilled you'd allow me to sit with you and have a cup of coffee."

Kacie smiled. "Well, I'm glad you cared enough to straighten it out. And my dad is really a great guy."

Bret said, "Oh, I'm sure he is." But he didn't mean it. "Kacie, I really don't mean to be forward, especially after I've given you my life story in three acts, but after I get a job, would you have dinner with me? I've really enjoyed talking with you."

"Well, why do you have to wait until then?"

"I'm old school. I believe it's my responsibility to pay for the meal."

"Why don't you let me buy your meal?"

"I couldn't do that," he said as he looked into her eyes. Looking into her eyes was more stimulating than looking into Angie's ever was.

"Well, I know what we could do, and it wouldn't cost any money," Kacie said as she raised her eyebrows.

"And what would that be?" Bret asked, also raising his eyebrows.

"Why don't you go to church with me this Sunday?"

"Wow. My dad had been after me to go with him, but I never did. What church do you attend?"

"Well, you had coffee with my pastor the last time I saw you here."

"He's my dad's pastor, too!" Bret said surprisingly.

Suddenly, Kacie had an astonishing look on her face. "John Davidson was your dad!? Oh, he was such a sweet man. Isn't that incredible? I've known your dad ever since he joined the church. I had planned to go to his funeral, but I had to get lunch for one of the other teachers because her kids had a bug that day and a fever."

"Wow, it sure is a small world," Bret said.

"So, to answer your question, yes, I would love to go to dinner with you. I just hope you find a job soon," Kacie said with a grin.

"And in answer to your question, I accept your invitation to church. Shall I pick you up or just meet you there?"

"Oh, for the first time, why don't we just meet there?"

"That'll be fine. Thank you so much, Kacie."

"Let me give you my number. We can keep in touch about Sunday."

"Thank you. I guess I'd better head out and find that job."

"And I have to hurry to make sure I'm in my classroom before the bell rings. I'm an elementary schoolteacher."

"Wow, I never knew Arnold Glassman had a daughter who was a teacher. And I never would have believed he had a daughter as beautiful as you."

"Aw, thank you. That's sweet. Well, I'll look forward to Sunday."

"Me too. I'll see you there."

Kacie and Bret walked out to their cars together. He sat in his car for a while after she pulled away. He was staring without really looking at anything. He was deep in thought.

"How could a creep like Glassman have a daughter like that? She might think he's a great guy, but I know he's a total scoundrel," Bret said out loud, with venom in every word. "I hope he gets his someday," he said as he drove out of the parking lot.

Standing at the curb as Bret pulled up to the stop sign was Harold. He just smiled and gave Bret a thumbs-up.

"Man, that's a strange dude," Bret said as he drove away.

Chapter Twelve

The Doctor Was Right

When Arnold opened his eyes, he couldn't believe it was 8:30. He had never been late to work a day in his life. He threw the covers back, sat upright on the side of the bed, and rubbed his eyes. Immediately, he began coughing. He could hardly make his way to the bathroom for a tissue. The discharge looked worse than before, and he had no energy. The doctor was right. This stuff was aggressive.

He picked up his phone and called the office.

"Mr. Glassman's office, may I help you?" his assistant said with a lot of cheer in her voice.

"Mrs. DeBarry, this is Arnold. I'm going to be a little late this morning. If I have any appointments, you'll have to reschedule them."

"Yes, Mr. Glassman. I was a little anxious when you didn't call me after your appointment yesterday."

"Oh, I'm sorry. I just got busy. I'm okay. He gave me some meds. Thank you for asking. I'll see you a little later this morning."

"I'm so glad to hear that. I was so worried about you. Don't worry about a thing. I'll take care of your appointments and see you later."

"Thank you, Mrs. DeBarry," Arnold said and ended the call.

He felt terrible and moved very slow. He skipped his paper and coffee and oatmeal and instead shaved and showered.

After his shower, he opened the dresser drawer and saw the handgun again. He closed his eyes and continued getting dressed.

He went to his kitchen table with a pad and pen. Slowly he began writing a to-do list.

1. Call the lawyer about a will.
2. Consider who will take over the company.
3. Fast-track the sale of the company.
4. Talk with Kacie.

The last one was the most difficult to write. Tears welled up in his eyes. He wiped them away and went to the pantry. His eyes zeroed in on a bottle of sleeping pills. He stared at it for a few seconds and closed the door. He couldn't believe the dark thoughts that were tempting him.

He sat at the table again and lamented, "Dear God, help me!" Then he put his head down and cried.

* * *

Harold turned to Peter. "He's not really considering what I think he's considering, is he?"

"Yes, he is. But you're going to make sure he doesn't."

"How am I going to do that?"

"Harold, I've been supporting you up until now. From here on out, though, you're going to have to make your own decisions about to how to help Arnold."

"Me?" Harold said with a big question mark on his face.

"Yes, you. I have the greatest confidence in you. I know you'll handle Arnold's situation just fine the rest of the way. You're on your own from this moment on."

"Are you sure? I mean, I might mess things up. What if I make a bad decision? I don't know, Peter!"

"Harold, look at me. You can do this, and we have confidence in you that you will do a great job. Now, I have other business to take care of. I'll be keeping an eye on you. And when the time comes, you'll have the *right touch*. Bless you, Harold."

* * *

Arnold entered his office through the back entrance so he wouldn't be bombarded with questions by anyone noticing his late arrival.

"Good morning, Mrs. DeBarry."

"Good morning, Mr. Glassman. Are you feeling all right? You look a little pale."

"Yes, I'm fine. It's probably the medication. Please call Jerry Blackburn and make an appointment for this afternoon. Don't take no for an answer. Remind him how much money he makes off of me and my company."

"Yes, Mr. Glassman."

"And tell Mr. McCarty to come to my office immediately."

"Yes, Mr. Glassman. Right away."

Back in his office, Arnold was racked with another coughing spell. He was exhausted as he sat at his desk. And his day had not even started.

"Mr. Glassman," Mrs. DeBarry interrupted, "Mr. McCarty is here to see you."

"Okay, send him in."

The CFO entered smiling. "I have an update on how the cutbacks are going. I'm pleased to say it has all been taken care of, and we'll begin to see an immediate difference financially for the company."

"We need to talk, Bill," Arnold interrupted. "I'm going to sell the company. But before I do, I need to—"

Immediately McCarty blurted out, "What! Why do you want to do that, Mr. Glassman? The buyer will bring in their own management and chief executives, and there'll be an audit." Then he added more boldly than he should have, "Mr. Glassman, *I'll* be out of a job!"

"I'm sick, Bill. Real sick. And—"

McCarty interrupted him again. "Then let me take over and run things, and you take it easy. I can run the company, and you can recuperate. I can run the company as well as you can, maybe even better."

While Arnold's first thoughts as to who should run the company had included McCarty, he didn't like what the CFO had said about his running the company possibly better than he had.

"You pompous little numbers cruncher. Do you realize who you're talking to?"

But McCarty didn't back down.

"Of course, I know whom I am talking to. And as your CFO, I'm telling you that you won't get what you think this company is worth if you try to sell it now."

"What makes you say that?"

"I've been holding back some information from you because you've seemed so distracted lately. I didn't think it would be good to bring it up. As you know, your stock has gone down considerably because our sales are down. You've got a skeleton workforce doing the jobs that forty more employees should be doing in addition to their own workload—"

"Wait a minute! Wait just a minute. You've been holding back information? I've trusted you to keep my company in the position it has been for many years, including before you were even out of grade school, and now you're telling me my company isn't in the shape you've been assuring me it was in?"

"You see, Mr. Glassman, you really need me now. Without my leadership and knowledge of where things are and who is doing what, this company will be in even worse shape. So I suggest you go home and let me run the company. I'll call you if I need you."

As soon as he finished the last sentence, McCarty got up and walked out of the office.

Arnold sat there with a look of horror on his face. Did that insolent, arrogant pencil pusher just tell him, the president of the company, that he was in charge?

Mrs. DeBarry interrupted his thoughts. "Mr. Glassman, Mr. Blackburn said you can call him any time this morning."

"Thank you, Mrs. DeBarry," Arnold said as another coughing spell began. "God, help me!" Arnold said as he put his head between his hands.

Before calling anyone, though, Arnold summoned the HR director and heard the whole story of what McCarty had done with the cutbacks and the way he carried them out. Arnold was not happy with what he heard.

Then he met with the heads of accounting and bookkeeping to get the full picture of where his company was financially. Again, he was not happy with what he learned.

McCarty had seemingly made himself indispensable through the unilateral decisions he had made regarding the company's resources and short-term plans. The department heads confirmed that McCarty's actions had placed everything under his immediate control. The only person who could overrule the CFO was Arnold. But his health was a greater impediment to Arnold's running the company than Bill McCarty. Arnold was going down fast, and he seemed to be stuck with Bill McCarty running his company.

Arnold felt depressed and, at that moment, powerless. He decided to seek the friendlier confines of his home to gather his thoughts and do what he thought he needed to do.

In the car as he drove home, he began to feel even weaker. His thoughts turned dark.

As soon as he walked through the door, his home phone rang. He didn't feel like answering, but he heard Kacie's voice as she began to leave a voice mail. "Dad, this is Kacie. I called the office, and Mrs. DeBarry said you weren't feeling well and had gone home."

He quickly picked up the phone. "Hey, baby. How are you doing?"

"No, Dad, the question is how are *you* doing?"

"I'm okay. Just not feeling as good as I normally do."

"Well, I'm nearby. Would it be okay to stop by for a few moments?"

Though Arnold wasn't ready to talk to her, he said, "Yes, baby, come on by."

When they ended the call, Arnold wondered if he should tell her about the cancer now or wait. Should he tell her about the company? Should he say anything about McCarty's maneuvering to take over everything and show him the door?

Before he could decide anything, Kacie entered and gave him a big hug.

"Dad, I'm sorry you're not feeling well, but I had to come over and tell you I've met someone."

Arnold wasn't expecting this. "You mean—"?

"Yes, Dad, believe it or not, I've met someone."

A spate of questions erupted from Arnold: "Who is he? How did you meet him? What does he do for a living? How long have you known him?"

"Dad, Dad, please. I'm trying to tell you all of that."

"Of course, baby, I'm sorry. Start at the beginning. I'm just a little surprised. All this time you've never had someone you thought enough to tell me about. I guess I'm new to all this."

"That's okay. I know I've never had a boyfriend to speak of before. I haven't known him that long, but—"

"Haven't known him that long. He could be an axe murderer. You don't know this man, Kacie!"

"Dad, I didn't say I'm going to marry him. I'm simply saying I've met someone I really like."

"Of course, dear. I'm sorry. You know I'm very protective when it comes to my baby girl."

"I know, Dad. I've never met anyone like Bret. He's got manners. He's smart. He's responsible—"

"You've determined all of that *and* you haven't known him that long? How in the world did you determine any of this?"

"Well, Dad, have you ever met someone you just seemed to click with? He's coming to church with me this Sunday. I'm looking forward to getting to know him better. Perhaps this is the man God has for me," she said and smiled.

"Well, Kacie, you're a smart woman. One of the smartest I've ever known. I hope this man turns out to be who you hope he is."

"Thank you, Dad. But *you'll* always be the greatest man in my life. You know that, don't you, Daddy?"

"Of course, I do, sweetheart."

"Dad, I'm so sorry. Here I am running on and on, but I need to take care of you. You're not feeling well. What is it? The flu? You look like you feel really bad."

"I'll be okay, sweetie. I'm taking my medicine. I'll be okay. Besides, I have to be well. I've got a business trip coming up that's going to take me away for a couple of weeks," Arnold said, making sure he would have a couple of weeks to make some very big decisions with minimum distractions. If he could make Kacie think he was going to be out of town, he'd be able to focus on the biggest decisions of his life.

"But, Dad, Christmas isn't that far away. You've never taken a trip this close to Christmas."

"I know, dear, but it's very important."

"Well, okay, but keep in touch the whole time." She saw again how weak he looked. "Are you sure you'll be able to make it? You really don't look well."

"I'll make it, sweetie. I'll make it."

"Well, I have to be going. I've got a bunch of papers to grade. Let me know if I can do anything to help you prepare for your trip," she said and kissed him on the forehead.

"Bye, dear, and remember, I love you a whole bunch!"

"Do you remember how much you used to tell me you loved me?"

"Yes, I do. A bushel and a peck and a hug around the neck!"

"Thanks, Daddy. You're so sweet. Bye-bye!"

As soon as Kacie closed the door, Arnold almost collapsed into a chair and his breathing quickened. When he finally caught his breath, he made a phone call.

"Jerry, this is Arnold Glassman. I need to get a lot done in a short time, and I don't need a lot of questions."

"Yes, Mr. Glassman. What can I do for you?

"First, I need you to draw up a will for me. I can't believe I haven't done that yet. I also need you to make sure my daughter gets everything."

"I can do that and ensure she will have minimal government interference."

"Thanks, Jerry. I know you can do that, and I appreciate you thinking like that. But regarding the business, I have to say Bill McCarty is making me very nervous. He's more or less taken over the company and put me in a bad position. I want to sell the company. What I need you to do is to make sure the company will sell for fair market price and protect me from that bloodsucking jackal."

"I understand, Mr. Glassman. To be honest, I've never liked McCarty. He always struck me as too pompous, arrogant, and condescending."

"Well, at least I know we're talking about the same man," Arnold quipped.

"Mr. Glassman, is everything okay? I've never heard you sound like this."

"Confidentially, Jerry, I'm not okay. My doctor has found an aggressive cancer, and he's estimated I've got about six weeks."

"I'm so sorry, Mr. Glassman. I'm so sorry. I'll do everything I can to take care of these things for you."

"Thank you, Jerry. I knew you would. Let me know how it goes. And, of course, this is all confidential."

"I understand, Mr. Glassman."

Arnold ended the call and began to pray out loud. "Lord, I can't go out this way. I can't just waste away in front of my baby. I can't do that . . . I just can't."

His thoughts turned dark again. How could he end his life on his own terms and yet avoid the appearance of suicide? He knew a person in his right mind wouldn't think like this. But he continued to puzzle out a way to die and avoid the scandal of self-destruction. Could he stage it to look like a home invasion gone awry? Surely Kacie could deal with that a lot better than if she knew he had taken his own life.

He would have to plan this very carefully.

Chapter Thirteen
Matchmaker, Matchmaker, Make Me a Match

Kacie went shopping for a new dress for Sunday. Though she had a closet full of nice dresses, she convinced herself there was nothing unusual about shopping for this new dress.

What was so special about Bret that she felt compelled to impress him with a new dress? There was nothing wrong with wanting to look nice for their church date, was there? No. There was nothing wrong with any of that she concluded as she held up a dress in front of a mirror.

When she found the right dress, she decided she needed a new pair of shoes to go with it. And there was nothing unusual about that. She had bought shoes to go with certain dresses before.

After she'd made her purchases, she visited a nearby coffee shop. She decided to relax and enjoy her coffee on one of the benches. But all the benches were partially occupied. Well, she didn't mind sharing a bench, as long the other person didn't make it awkward. She didn't have to worry about that, though, because a moment after she sat down, the person at the other end of the bench gathered her things and left.

Kacie checked her bags for a second. When she looked up, a man sat down and joined her on the bench.

"Hello," he greeted her. "My name is Harold. May I share this bench with you?"

"Yes, please," Kacie said. "I'm just taking a short break. I'm Kacie."

"What do you do for a living, Kacie?"

"I'm a schoolteacher."

"Wow, you must have a lot of patience."

"Well, that's part of it."

"Are you married?"

"No," she slowly answered.

"Oh, I don't mean to be nosy. I just love to talk to people and find out about their lives. I hope you don't mind."

"No, no problem," Kacie said as she sipped her coffee.

"Marriage is a great thing, though, isn't it?" Harold said.

"I don't really know," she said. "I've never been married."

"I think marriage is one of God's greatest gifts. The opportunity to spend a lifetime with someone you love. To have children and watch them grow up."

"That sounds great. Hopefully I'll find out someday."

"You know," Harold said. "I was a firefighter, and I guess I let my job consume me. If I could do it all over again, I would have spent more time with someone special."

"Oh, I'm so sorry. Has your wife passed away?" Kacie asked as she placed a hand on Harold's arm.

"Well . . . well, you could say that," Harold stammered, trying to think of a good answer.

"That sounds so sweet," she said. "But you can still look for a special someone again, can't you?"

"No, Kacie, it'll never happen for me. And believe me, it's okay. I know God has other things for me to do. If you don't mind me asking, are you seeing anyone special?"

"You know, it's a little strange you should ask that. I've met someone I just seem to click with. He's coming to church with me this Sunday. I'm very excited about it."

"That's great. Church is a great place to meet someone. After all, it was God who invented marriage and gave us the Book on how it's supposed to function. If we do it God's way, it's amazing how it works out."

"Wow, for a retired firefighter, you seem to have a lot of insight into these things."

"Thank you. I really felt that God wanted me to sit with you and encourage you. And I believe He wanted me to tell you to trust your heart. Thank you for letting me share this bench with you."

"You're more than welcome. I was a little hesitant when we first started talking, but you've said some things that really helped me. Thank you for sharing them with me."

"Before I go, Kacie, if you find that special someone, don't let him get away. Trust your heart. Just trust your heart. I'll say a prayer for you. Thank you again," Harold said as he got up and walked away.

Kacie thought to herself, "Wow. I meant to relax for a moment, but I couldn't get Bret off my mind. Then this man sat down beside me and talked about the things that are on my mind. This truly was a God thing."

Kacie felt her heart was at peace about Bret. She threw away her cup, gathered her bags, and headed for her car. This had been a great day for her.

* * *

Bret's day, however, wasn't going well at all. He'd received rejections all day long from every job opportunity he'd sought out. No one was interested now but maybe in January. When he got home, he found an envelope from Glassman Industries. In addition to a check, there was a letter:

> I regret to inform you our records show
> you did not have as much vacation time
> as you indicated. Thus the enclosed check
> is for an amount less than you anticipated.

> For economic reasons, we will not be able to provide two months' health insurance coverage from the date of termination. Therefore, your insurance will expire after one month. Please review the attached COBRA information.

The letter bore Arnold Glassman's electronic signature. Bret knew he had the vacation time he had entered on his exit form, but he figured it wasn't a fight worth fighting. The few dealings he had with Glassman Industries were too many anyway.

"Glassman has got to be one of the worst people on the face of the world," Bret said out loud as he filed the letter to reread later. "He's got a big house and a big car and all the money anyone could ever need. And yet, he has the nerve to treat people who have given him their blood, sweat, and tears like used toilet paper. He just uses them and flushes them away. He wouldn't know fair if it came up and slapped him upside his head. Kacie must have been adopted because there's no way someone as nice as her came from his bloodline."

When he thought of Kacie, he thought about their church date, and he felt slightly uncomfortable. Whether she was adopted or not, he couldn't separate her from Arnold Glassman. Maybe it would be better not to join her at church this weekend. He decided to call her and cancel, but the call went to her voice mail.

"This is Kacie. Leave a message and I'll call you back. Have a blessed day!"

"Kacie, this is Bret. Call me when you can. Thanks."

Bret went outside for some fresh air. As he looked into the sky, he heard a familiar voice.

"Hi, Bret. It's a lovely day, isn't it?" Harold said as he joined him in looking up at the sky.

Bret inwardly groaned at the appearance of the peculiar man again. "I guess it depends on whose perspective it is if it's a lovely day. Frankly, I've had better days."

"Well, maybe that'll change before the day is over," Harold said with a smile.

"What's your name?" Bret asked.

"Harold. And I believe God sent me to encourage you today."

"Encourage me?" Bret said with an air of sarcasm in his voice. "That'd be a switch. My dad died, my fiancée broke our engagement, I lost my job, and it looks like I won't find another until next year. Do you really think God gives two hoots about me, much less sending anyone to encourage me?"

"Well, Bret, sometimes God does things to get our attention and sometimes He has better things in store for us."

Bret's eyes opened a little wider. "You know, Harold, you're the second person who's told me that. I had a pastor say the same thing to me."

"Well, I don't know what's going through your mind, but the best thing to do is to just go and talk with the person who can change things for you. You can't change your dad's dying. You can't change your fiancée's mind. So maybe the best thing is to go talk to your boss."

"I really appreciate your encouragement, Harold—"

"See, I did encourage you!"

"Yeah, I really appreciate that, but the chances of my former boss talking to me are pretty much slim and none."

"Well, I can't make you go, Bret. But it would be a lot better than stealing from him," Harold said with a chuckle as he walked off.

"Steal from him?" Bret muttered as he walked back into the house.

A few minutes later his phone rang, and he saw it was Kacie calling. How could he get out of this?

"Hello, this is Bret," he said.

"Hi, Bret. This is Kacie. How're you doing?" she asked cheerfully.

"Well, to be honest, it hasn't been the best of days."

"I'm sorry to hear that. I forgot to tell you that the service starts at eleven. I thought I should tell you that before I forgot. You're still coming, right?"

Bret stammered and cleared his throat.

"You're still coming, aren't you?" she asked again.

"Yeah. Of course, I'll be there. I'm really looking forward to it," Bret said, not knowing what else to say. "We didn't say anything about lunch, but I've got a gift card for Olive Garden. Would you like to go there afterward?"

"Sure, that sounds nice. I really like their soup and salad."

"Okay. I'll get to the church around ten forty-five. Can I meet you out front?"

"Sure, that'll work. I look forward to seeing you then. See you Sunday!" she said with an incredibly cheerful inflection in her voice.

"Okay, I'll see you then!"

The call ended and Bret stared at his phone for a moment, waiting for the uneasiness in his chest to go away. Still, he told himself, he never really wanted to cancel. He realized Kacie had somehow found a place in his heart.

CHAPTER FOURTEEN

I Love It When a Plan Comes Together

Harold was waiting for Peter and playing an imaginary game of ticktacktoe. Peter appeared with a strange look on his face.

"Harold, what are you doing?"

"Oh, sorry, Peter. I was working through my plan to help Arnold. And to be honest, I wanted to run some things by you and make sure they're all right."

"There's no reason to run anything by me. I trust your judgment. I'm sure you're doing a great job."

"I just thought it would be a good idea to—"

"Harold, there is no reason. I'm sure you're doing a good job."

"Peter, I wish I had as much confidence in me as you. I've never done anything like this before, and I want to do these people right."

"Do you remember when the fire chief specifically told you to come up with a plan for incoming firefighters? Do you recall how jealous the other guys were that the chief gave you that job and not them?"

"Yes, I do. I hadn't thought about that in a long time. I remember asking why he chose me to do that."

"And what did the chief say to you?"

"He said that I was one of the best firefighters in the department, and they wanted the best to come up with the plan."

"That's right. And you did come up with a plan, and you did it well, with excellence."

"But that's a lot different than what I'm doing now," said Harold.

"I think you're looking at the situation and making the necessary adjustments, at least that's what I saw you doing when I walked in. That's all I'm asking of you, Harold. Just do your best!"

"I'm trying. But the plan doesn't just involve Arnold; it also involves Bret Davidson."

"Ah, yes, Bret. He's a good man. I can see how you would want to involve him. I think that's great that you would plan it out like this.

"You mean you know what I'm going to do?"

"Not everything, Harold. But I know you'll do a great job. And I'm sure you'll have *just the right touch*! Now, I really must be going. There are some others I have to meet with."

"Okay, Peter. Thank you for your confidence. I won't do anything to let you down," Harold said. Then, he thought, "Well, it's time to start the countdown. We'll see if all his confidence works. I wonder what he meant by just the right touch."

* * *

Bret was feeling a little nervous as he pulled into the church parking lot. He was rehearsing some lines for when he saw Kacie, but before he could finish, someone knocked at his window. Kacie looked absolutely stunning. He smiled and got out.

"You look awesome!" he said and blushed a little.

"Why, thank you, Bret. You look very handsome. Let's go inside and find a seat."

It had been a long time since Bret had been to church. And he had never been to a Baptist church, so he was a little nervous about the whole thing. Hopefully, they wouldn't bring out the snakes until he was gone. Why did he think they had snakes? Maybe the snake thing was just in Appalachia. Maybe they weren't even Baptist. Maybe they didn't do anything with snakes. Maybe he should just stop thinking about snakes.

As they walked into the church, several people smiled and greeted Kacie and Bret. At the least, he thought, they seemed friendly and normal. Maybe this wouldn't be as bad as he feared.

During the first part of the worship service, the music sounded great. This was far different than what he anticipated. Some of the people on the platform had instruments, but most of them were vocalists. The music seemed really upbeat.

One of the worship leaders said, "I love this season. Christmas is my favorite time of the year. How about you?" Several people said *amen* and most clapped. "Listen to this song by Mark Lowry, 'Mary Did You Know?'"

The leader had a great voice, and he sang a song Bret had never heard. He listened intently to the message of the song. When he looked at Kacie, he saw she had closed her eyes and was taking in everything the guy was singing.

The other music was equally uplifting, and everyone sang most of the songs. After a while, the pastor got up to deliver his message. "Christmas is one of the most difficult times of the year for some people. This Christmas will be the first time some will celebrate it without a loved one."

That certainly touched Bret's heart, and he looked down. Kacie noticed this and put her hand on his hand and gave it a squeeze. Bret understood she meant this as an encouragement.

Pastor McDowell continued with a message of hope because of the greatest gift God had ever given, His only Son, Jesus. "God stepped out of heaven and into a manger, and the world hasn't been the same since."

Bret loved the message and realized it was relevant to him. When the pastor concluded the message, there was a time for people to respond. Bret held back, but he was very observant as other people responded.

After the service, he and Kacie made their way out of the church. Pastor McDowell was shaking hands at the exit.

"Bret, it's so good to see you. I hope you felt welcomed today. I also hope you will come back again. And Kacie, thank you for sitting with Bret today to make him feel welcomed."

"Well, Pastor, we actually met that day you and Bret met at Starbucks."

"That's right. I remember seeing you come in. Well, thank you for inviting him. I also invited him, but maybe you made a better impression on him than I did," the pastor said with a chuckle.

"No, Pastor, I've been planning to attend for some time. Kacie invited me to her church, but I had no idea she meant this church. When I found out this was Dad's church, I couldn't turn her down. I really enjoyed the service, and I will definitely be back."

"God bless you, Bret. You made my day! You two have a great rest of the day!"

"Thank you, Pastor. We will."

Bret opened the car door for Kacie. As he walked around to the driver's side, he couldn't believe he was so quickly becoming attracted to her. But he told himself he couldn't do that. She was Arnold Glassman's daughter, and he *hated* Arnold. How could he possibly keep this up? It would never work.

As they were pulling out of the parking area, Kacie said, "Bret, thank you so much for attending church with me. I have several friends in this church, but I've always felt a little lonely on Sundays. I usually don't sit with anyone. It was great today to have someone to sit with."

"You know, I had no idea what to expect. But I really enjoyed the service. It brought a lot of questions to mind that I need to answer. Hopefully, I'll have coffee with the pastor again."

"There's the Olive Garden," Kacie said, thinking Bret was going to drive past it.

"Sorry, I was caught up in our conversation."

He parked and walked around to open the door for her. That certainly made a good impression. They entered the restaurant and had only a short wait before a hostess showed them to a table. They both ordered the soup and salad combo.

Bret was amazed at how easy it was to talk to Kacie. She was an extraordinary woman, even if she was Arnold Glassman's daughter.

"So, how is your dad doing?" he asked with as much sincerity as he could muster.

"He's been ill lately. To be honest, I'm worried about him. He's supposed to be away for a while on a business trip, but I wasn't thrilled with the news, especially since Christmas is so near."

Arnold was going to be out of town? Suddenly Bret remembered the strange man saying something about stealing. Why would he say such a thing? Bret wasn't a thief.

"Do you have any plans for Christmas, Bret?"

Bret barely heard her over his thoughts. He didn't have plans, and though he really wanted to see what she had in mind, he couldn't let her suggest anything.

"I'm supposed to go to a friend's house. His family invited me a long time ago. They'd be very disappointed if I didn't show up."

"I understand," Kacie said with a hint of disappointment.

After the meal and more conversation, they were in the parking lot. Again, he opened the door for her and drove her back to the church parking lot. The only car there was a Mustang. "Man, that is a sweet-looking car!" he said, smiling.

"Yes, that's it."

"I love Mustangs. I've always wanted one."

"Well, if you play your cards right, I just might let you drive it one day," Kacie said with a smile.

"Well, we'll see. Thank you so much, Kacie, for inviting me. I had a really nice time," Bret said as he walked her to her car.

"Me too," she said. "I really enjoyed it, too."

Kacie hoped Bret would ask when they might get together again, but he didn't. He only said, "You're a very precious woman. And it was an honor to be with you today. I hope you have a great rest of the day."

"Thank you, Bret. You too."

And that was it. Bret walked back to his car. Kacie felt a little hurt with the way their time together ended. But she thought he might call her later and make another date.

Bret drove out of the parking lot, mentally mapping the route to Arnold Glassman's neighborhood. He knew the exclusive neighborhood well and was sure he could find the Glassman house. But then he asked himself why he wanted to drive by the house. Yet, he could still hear Kacie's voice, telling him that her father would be out of town for a while.

Bret drove slowly into the neighborhood, scanning the houses from side to side. Finally, he saw the Glassman name on a mailbox. It was a large home. He didn't see any security system signs or stickers around the property or displayed on the house. That was a plus. He parked a couple of houses down from the Glassman house and walked back. He took notice of the front entry, the garage door, a door on the side of the garage, and the windows facing the street as well as those on the side. Was there an out-of-the-way entry point? Something not easily seen from the street?

Suddenly, he stopped, gathered his senses, and walked back to his car. What was he thinking? Who put this idea in his head? He'd never do anything like this. Break into someone's home? Why could he not stop thinking about this? Why did he continually hear the odd man's parting words about robbing his former boss?

Chapter Fifteen

Doing What You Shouldn't to Do What You Should

Bret sat at his dining table, staring out the window while Christmas music played on the radio. He couldn't believe he was really thinking about doing the unthinkable.

He was obsessed, telling himself how Arnold Glassman had ruined people's lives. How Arnold Glassman had ruined *his* life. What kind of man fired people just before Christmas? "I gave him five years of my life," he said out loud to no one. "I always did the best job anyone could do. And after he fired me without cause, he then cheated me out of my vacation time and ended my health insurance! This is all Glassman's fault. I'm sure he's got a few things that would help me make it until I get another job."

Bret was talking himself into actually breaking into someone else's home. Breaking and entering and stealing. How many crime dramas could he replay in his memory? Better to make a mental list than write anything down that might betray him later. He started to plan the break-in.

"There's no alarm system. Glassman is out of town. The timing has to be perfect. I'll steal from the rich to help the poor—namely, me!"

* * *

Arnold was laboring to breathe. His strength was gone. Without it, he couldn't imagine how he could trash his home to make it look like a break-in. He'd seen enough "CSI" episodes to know the authorities would figure out a phony scene.

He made sure Jerry had all of his final instructions. Even though crooked Bill McCarty was now running things at the company, he'd be taken care of after Arnold was gone. The company would be sold, and all the assets would go to Kacie.

Arnold had to write her a letter. He sat down with a legal pad and pen. He hoped he could at least give her some comfort in writing.

> Dear precious daughter,
> You have always been my sunshine for any dark day I faced. I've never cared what happened to me. I've only been concerned for you.

I've been diagnosed with a fast-growing, aggressive cancer. The doctor told me my time was short, but even he had no idea it would be this short.

I couldn't bear the thought of you watching me slowly die. Even though I am taking my own life, I was going to die very soon. I guess that's not the best rationalization, but it's the best I can do.

I have taken care of all the details, so you won't be bothered with the company. Jerry Blackburn has all the information you'll need. You can trust him. Likewise, you can trust Mrs. DeBarry. But stay away from Bill McCarty. Don't trust anything he says.

I'm so deeply sad that I won't get to walk you down the aisle when you get married. I only hope the man you choose will make you the happiest woman on earth. You deserve the best.

I love you, dear, sweet, precious baby girl.

Arnold's eyes filled with tears as he reread the note.

* * *

Bret parked his car outside Arnold's gated community. He moved around to the back of the property and approached the Glassman house from the woods. All of his senses were on edge, hoping no one would see him. His heart was pounding. He thought he could hear it beating as he entered the backyard. He feared others might hear it, too.

His eyes widened with surprise when he looked through the door at the back of the garage and saw a car. "Yikes! Is he home? Why is he home?" After a few moments, Bret set himself at ease, reasoning his nemesis hadn't driven himself to the airport. "Maybe he took a cab. Maybe Kacie took him. There're plenty of reasons why his car is here," he surmised.

Bret's gloved hand tried the doorknob. It was open! "Mr. Big Shot, Fancy Pants forgot to lock his backdoor. Maybe I should thank him later," he smirked. He entered the garage and quickly found the door into the house. His heart rate jumped up another gear or two.

Arnold was sitting, staring at the gun on the coffee table. Every nerve in his body was on edge. All he could do was think about Kacie. The letter was cowardly. He felt cowardly. He felt ashamed. Tears streamed down his cheeks. "Wouldn't the gun make a mess? Should I reconsider the pills?" he wondered.

Bret walked carefully into the kitchen, keeping his flashlight down so as to avoid drawing attention from outside. "Now, if I were a fat cat like Glassman," he pondered, "where would I keep my valuables?" The bedroom was the best place to start. And after checking that out, he'd look for a study or a den.

He found a set of stairs just beyond the kitchen. He walked stealthily to the second floor and noticed several doors leading into individual rooms. The first door was a guest room. The next seemed to be an office. Bret made a mental note to check it after he finished going through the bedroom. He checked the next door. Bingo! The master suite.

The first thing he saw as he looked around was a huge portrait of Kacie on the wall. She wore a beautiful evening gown and looked like a million dollars. Bret stared at the painting and his heart sank. Her eyes immediately struck him, piercing him like a thousand knives. Those eyes seemed to look into his very soul. He was frozen with guilt and shame.

"What am I doing here?" he whispered.

Suddenly his conscience screamed at him to come to his senses. "Stop this! You're no thief! It not too late to get out of here and forget you ever thought about doing something so stupid, so wrong, so craven!" He could simply leave. No one would be the wiser for what he had done and almost done.

Bret exited the bedroom. He decided to take the stairs at the far end. But why was there a light on below? Maybe Glassman's lamps were on timers. He slipped down the stairs and caught a glimpse of the immaculate living room—and Arnold Glassman.

Bret's heart rate spiked so hard he thought it would burst out of his chest. A thousand questions pummeled his mind. *What should I do? What should I say? Is there any way out of here? Has he seen me? Has he already called the police?*

He pressed his back against the wall. Glassman's back was toward him. Maybe he could sneak back up the stairs and out the back way before anyone knew he'd been there.

But he didn't move. He just stood there. Looking at the man who'd wrecked his life. While he knew he shouldn't be there, he sensed something strange about the moment for Arnold Glassman. Then he saw the gun.

Arnold picked up the letter and read it again. He stared at the gun. He put the letter on the coffee table and reached for the gun. He stopped. He picked up the letter again. After a few seconds, his body was racked with sobs. He put the letter down and let his head fall onto his chest and cried.

Bret froze. But his mind went into overdrive. "He's got a gun! Did he hear me! He's got a gun! He's going to shoot a home invader! He's got a gun! He's going to shoot me! He's got a gun!" Bret wanted to call out and beg for his life. But he couldn't move, couldn't make a sound. He could only watch Arnold.

He saw Arnold lift the gun.

He's going to shoot me! He's going to shoot me!

But Arnold never looked toward him. Instead, he turned the gun toward . . . himself!

Bret's mind was spinning. He had to do something. But if he stopped Arnold, Arnold might shoot him. At the least, he'd surely have him arrested. His mind raced as Arnold pointed the gun toward his head.

I've got to do something!

Finally Bret shouted, "No, Mr. Glassman! You can't do that!"

Arnold dropped the gun. Fortunately, it didn't go off. With what little strength he had, he turned toward the voice. His eyes widened. "Who the devil are you? What are you doing in my house?"

Bret had no choice but to surrender and face the music. He'd broken into the house with the intent to steal, but he'd also just stopped a suicide. At least, it looked like a suicide. He could beg for forgiveness. Maybe he'd be able to go home tonight. And maybe he wouldn't have to worry about where he'd be living for the next ten or fifteen years or need to apply for any more jobs.

He slowly approached Arnold. As he looked into his eyes he could tell something was wrong with him. He looked weak and desperate.

"May I sit down and talk to you before you call the cops?"

"To be honest with you, kid, I don't have enough energy to keep you from doing anything you want to do. You could steal everything in the house, and I wouldn't be able to stop you."

"I'm Bret Davidson. I used to work for you . . . that is, before you fired me last week through that weasel, your CFO, McCarty."

"Yeah," Arnold grinned. "I agree with you. He's a full-blooded weasel. I wish I'd never met him!"

"Tell me about it, Mr. Glassman. But this is about more than my job. You see, my dad died almost a week ago. While we'd drifted apart over the last few years, I can't tell you how much I miss him now. There are so many things I want to say to him, should have said to him. And now I can't. But I know this about you. You have the most wonderful daughter in the world! I can't imagine how she'd feel about you taking your life tonight. Mr. Glassman, do you have any idea how wonderful she is?"

"Of course I do!" Arnold said with tears in his eyes. "But I'd rather die now than let her watch me die a little every day until it's all over. I have cancer. I don't want my baby to see me die that kind of death. A bullet or a bunch of pills is more merciful for her sake."

"Mr. Glassman, she's probably the most caring person I've ever met. If she knew you were hurting, she'd be here with you, helping you, comforting you, and hounding every doctor in the country to treat you."

"I take it you've met my sweet, precious daughter. You seem to know her. But that doesn't explain why you're here. What *are* you doing in my house *tonight*?"

"Well, sir, it's a long story. You see, this has been the worst week of my life. First, I lost my dad. Second, and this is going to sound a little strange, because I'm so smitten with Kacie right now, but I was engaged for almost a year, and my fiancée dumped me the night of my dad's funeral. And third, the day after my dad's funeral, that jerk McCarty fired me and had me escorted out of the building. I felt like a criminal. I've spent the last few days trying to find a job, but no one's hiring before Christmas—thank you very much, by the way, for that bit of timing. I've hit bottom.

In fact, I have to look up to see the bottom! I'm in despair . . . sorta like you." Bret paused.

"I made a rash decision this afternoon. I decided to steal from you to help me get through the holiday season. I needed to do something to keep my house and food on the table until I find another job. But a few minutes ago, I entered your bedroom and saw Kacie's portrait. Her picture brought me to my senses."

"Well, that painting has made me do some things I needed to do, too," Arnold said softly.

"Mr. Glassman, regardless of my situation, I shouldn't have broken into your house."

"Broke in? You idiot, the backdoor was unlocked! I left it open so my attorney could come in and find me!"

"No, no. That's not what I mean. I entered your home uninvited. You know, breaking and entering. But I have to say, I think I was supposed to be here tonight. A peculiar guy has been hanging around my neighborhood this week, and he said something to me about stealing from you. I know that sounds strange, but that's how the power of suggestion works. And even if the cops haul me away tonight, I'm glad I was here. I'm glad I stopped you from throwing away God's wonderful gift of life."

"I still don't want Kacie to watch me die bit by bit."

"If you really think about it, Mr. Glassman, I think that should be her decision. Don't you think she should be allowed to make that choice?"

There was a pause. "Well, I'm beginning to think you're right. About that and about why you're here. Would you help me get outside? I need some fresh air."

"Sure. I could use some, too."

Bret helped Arnold out of the chair. Arnold put his arm around him, and they walked toward the door. Outside, Arnold tried to take a slow breath to keep from coughing, but a coughing spasm ensued nonetheless. When it passed, the two men noticed a man approaching them.

Arnold said, "I remember you. You're that angel guy outside my doctor's office."

"This is the man I was telling you about. He suggested I should steal from you," Bret said.

Harold responded, "Well, if you'll remember, I said that talking with Arnold would be a lot better than stealing from him."

"Yeah, that's right. I remember."

"And you did talk with Arnold."

"Well, I never thought it would be like it was today, but I'm glad I got to talk with Mr. Glassman."

"Well, buddy—" said Arnold.

"My name is Harold."

"Well, Harold, you weren't a very good prophet with me."

"What do you mean?" Harold asked.

"You told me everything was going to be okay. And since then, nothing has been okay."

Harold paused and pondered a moment. Then he remembered Peter saying that he would have "just the right touch." He looked at his right hand and saw his palm begin to glow. He smiled and placed his hand on Arnold's shoulder. Immediately, Arnold's labored breathing became better and his color returned. Arnold felt a sudden strength surge through his body. He might not be able to leap tall buildings, but he felt like jumping for joy.

"I know this sounds strange, but I don't think I've ever felt this good. Maybe I'm taking a turn for the better," he said.

"In more ways than one, Arnold. In more ways than one," Harold said. And suddenly he vanished.

Bret stood there, stunned. "Did you see that? He just disappeared!"

"Yes," said Arnold. "He does that every time I see him. It doesn't strike me as strange anymore."

Arnold turned and walked back to his front door. "Come back inside with me, Bret. We need to talk a little more." He motioned for Bret to follow him.

"You need to call the police. If it's okay with you, I'll wait out here. I won't go anywhere until they get here."

"Nonsense. Come on in. My chairs are more comfortable for what we have to discuss."

Back inside, Arnold asked, "Tell me, why did McCarty let you go?"

"He said I wasn't important, or rather my position wasn't important. I told him I had made a couple of suggestions to my supervisor about some changes that would save the company a lot of money, but my supervisor took my ideas and presented them as his own. After that,

I kept my ideas to myself. I mean, I've been with the company for five years, and my managers have demanded I contribute more than my job, but they don't offer any opportunities for advancement. So I've been hesitant to volunteer any more ideas."

"Are you talking about the changes we made in shipping last year?"

"Yes, sir."

"McCarty told me that was his idea—" Arnold stopped before he said anything more about the CFO. "Bret, I'm sorry that happened. You should know he's been doing a lot of things I had no idea he was doing. I found out recently he's been taking advantage of me. I'm going to make some changes this week, beginning with Mr. McCarty. But I want to ask if you'd be interested in coming back and working for me again?"

"Sure, Mr. Glassman. I'd love that."

"What's your training?"

"I have a bachelor's in finance and an MBA in management and operations."

"Hmm," Arnold said and touched his chin. "And exactly how do you know my daughter with whom you're so smitten?"

"I met her the day after I was fired. Actually, I was meeting with her pastor and our paths crossed. He was my dad's pastor, and I later found out he was her pastor, too. But we didn't start out that well. I told her she was too beautiful to have a father like you. I called you a total creep. Sorry. I guess I'm the real creep here," he paused. "Do you want to call the police now?"

Arnold chuckled. "No. So you're the one Kacie was telling me about."

"Kacie mentioned me?"

Arnold nodded.

"We went to church together this morning and out to eat afterward. I probably didn't leave her thinking the best thoughts when we said good-bye. I had started planning to rob you, and I didn't think it would be a good idea to see her again. You probably want to call the police now."

"No, but I will if you say that one more time."

"Yes, sir. You know, I really did enjoy going to church with her. She's the most wonderful woman I've ever met. Would it be okay if I called on her again?"

"Maybe I will call the police now," Arnold said with a straight face. But then he smiled. "Just kidding."

"If you don't mind, Mr. Glassman, I'd appreciate it if we could keep this little meeting to ourselves." Bret stopped and thought for a second. "You know, she wanted to talk to you about getting my job back, but I asked her not to. I guess that was pride. And, as strange as it sounds, I think it was meant for me to be here tonight. That peculiar guy, Harold, made this all happen."

"Yes, Bret. I believe you're right," Arnold said. And then his eyes widened. "I don't think I've coughed in thirty minutes. I haven't even wheezed. I feel like my old self! I'm going to call my doctor first thing tomorrow and see what's going on. And I'll get your number from HR and tell you where I'm going to put you in the company. You can let yourself out." Arnold smiled at Bret. "And I won't say anything to Kacie about tonight, but if it's okay with you, I am going to tell Kacie that we've met and talked."

"Sure thing, Mr. Glassman."

Changing his mind about Bret letting himself out, Arnold said, "I don't know about you, but I'm as hungry as a bear. How about you? Are you any good in the kitchen? Let's start with a couple of sandwiches. And let's just talk. I want to know everything about you."

For the next couple of hours, the two talked and noshed. Arnold observed that Bret had a keen business mind and thought he might be a diamond in the rough, just the sort of person he wanted in an executive position.

After a while, Bret went home and wondered if this night had been real.

On Monday morning, Arnold met with Dr. Martin. He couldn't believe his ears as he listened to Arnold's lungs. He ordered a full battery of tests, none of which indicated there was any cancer in his patient. But Arnold could have told him that, and he pondered the healing power of Harold's touch.

Chapter Sixteen
What a Day!

"Kacie, this is Bret, do you have some time to talk?"

"I guess so. After the way you left me in the parking lot yesterday, I didn't think we'd be talking again."

"I know. I'm sorry about that. I don't have an excuse other than I was distracted with all that's going on. But you know, a couple of guys told me either God was trying to get my attention or else He had something better for me. And I have to tell you, they were right on both counts. I can't tell you how much better I feel today. Maybe ten or twelve years from now, I'll tell you everything I've been through in the last twenty-four hours."

"Ten or twelve years? How do you know what's going to happen that far in advance?"

"I know one thing: I've never met anyone like you before. And unless you tell me to go away, you're not going to get rid of me very easily."

"Wow, I've never had a guy tell me that before."

"Kacie, I had a chance last night to talk with your dad."

"What?"

"Yes, and he's not the jerk I said he was. I was wrong about him. We had a great conversation, and he's planning to hire me back!"

"I'm glad the two of you worked it out."

"Can I meet you at church this Sunday?"

"Yes, but this time you can pick me up at my house."

"I'd love to. I have a lot to do today. Your dad's supposed to call me later. Can I call you after that?"

"How about I call you after school."

"That sounds great! Bye."

* * *

As Arnold walked into his office, he realized he'd been doing something he hadn't done in a long time—smiling and saying hello to everyone he saw. Most of them replied with quizzical looks.

"Hello, Mrs. DeBarry. How are you today?" he said with a strong voice.

"Good morning, Mr. Glassman. You look so much better! That medicine must really be working!"

"To be honest, I feel like a million bucks! Please tell Mr. McCarty I'd like to see him in my office immediately."

"Yes, sir. And I'm so glad you're feeling better. I was worried. How did you get better so quickly?"

"Well, Mrs. DeBarry, I'll fill you in on that in about ten or twelve years."

Arnold made several calls to the department heads to let them know he was feeling better and that he was about to make some significant changes. As soon as he rang off with the head of HR, Bill McCarty knocked on his door.

"Yes, come in, Bill."

"Mr. Glassman, I thought we both understood there's no need for you to be here. Why don't you go home and leave everything to me?"

"No, Bill. I'm feeling great. In fact, I've changed my mind about selling the company. A fresh wind has blown across my bow, and I'm going to be making some changes of my own."

"Changes, Mr. Glassman? What kind of changes?"

"Frankly, Bill, they're none of your business. But when I want you to know, I'll let you. Now, get out of my office. I'm going to run my own company, if you don't mind."

"Mr. Glassman, you have no idea—"

"I have a complete grasp of the situation, and I told you to get out of my office. Don't make me repeat myself again!" Arnold said.

"Yes, Mr. Glassman. But if you need to know anything, I'll be in my office," McCarty said as he exited.

"That little toad has no idea what's about to happen," Arnold mumbled to himself.

He told Mrs. DeBarry to contact the department heads and let them know there would be an executive board meeting first thing the next morning. Then he called Bret.

"Bret, this is Arnold Glassman. We're having a meeting first thing tomorrow morning. I need you to be here bright and early. I'll be introducing you to all the department heads."

"Well, Mr. Glassman, a few of them already know me. Just tell me which department I'll be working in, and I'll be there ready for work."

"Did you hear me say that I would introduce you?"

"Yes, sir, I'm sorry. I'll be there bright and early."

"Good, we're going to have a great day tomorrow. I'll see you then."

Bret was perplexed. He'd never been to a meeting of all the department heads. Why did he need to attend one now? Well, he would find out soon enough.

His phone buzzed, and he saw it was Kacie.

"Hey, I just got off the phone with your dad. He wants me there first thing tomorrow morning."

"Wow, Bret, that's wonderful. Did he say what you'll be doing?"

"No. He said he was going to introduce me to the department heads. I have no idea what that is about."

"Well, my dad is a great judge of people. He must have something very important in mind."

"I'll bet Bill McCarty will be shocked to see me."

"Let me take back that thing about him being a great judge of people. He's not perfect. Mr. McCarty is evidence of that."

"This is so amazing. I worked for your dad for five years, and he didn't even know my name."

"Well, I know it will be a great day for you."

"That's what your dad said."

"Bret, I'm going Christmas shopping. Why don't you meet me at the mall?"

"How did you know I was behind in my shopping? I'll meet you at the coffee shop. Maybe we could have a cup in honor of our dads.

"That sounds great. I'll see you there."

A short time later, Bret and Kacie were talking over coffee. They walked all over the mall and talked. They shopped all over the mall and talked. They sat on a bench and talked. Bret couldn't believe how much his life had changed in such a short time. Kacie had captured his heart, and Arnold had changed his outlook on life.

He walked her to her car as he carried her bags. He put the bags in the trunk and opened her door for her. Then he just stood there, gazing into her eyes and smiling.

"You're amazing! Thank you for a wonderful day. You know I really hadn't gotten into the Christmas mood until now."

"Thank you for meeting me. I had a wonderful time, too. I'll pray for you about tomorrow. I'm sure you'll be a hit with the department heads."

"Thanks," Bret said, feeling lost in her eyes. Then there was silence as they studied each other. He leaned forward, and they kissed. "Good night. Be careful going home. I'll call you tomorrow and let you know how it went."

"I'll look forward to it, Bret. You be careful, too."

Bret walked, or rather floated, toward his car.

CHAPTER SEVENTEEN

What Goes Around

Bret could hardly sleep. He woke up before his alarm went off. He dressed and ate breakfast and was out the door.

He had never been in Arnold Glassman's office in the five years he had worked for him. When he walked into the building, a security guard brought everything to a standstill.

"Hey, whoa, where do you think you're going?"

"I have a meeting with Mr. Glassman. He's expecting me," Bret said confidently.

"Wait right here. I need to confirm this," he said and picked up the phone. "Mrs. DeBarry, this is Joe Thomas at the security desk. I've got a former employee here, and he says he has an appointment with Mr. Glassman. Okay, I'll ask him. What's your name, buddy?"

"Bret Davidson," he said, feeling his feet touch down on the ground.

After the security guard relayed the information, he said, "Really?" in a quizzical way and looked Bret over, up and down. "Okay, I'll send him up."

Bret noticed a marked change in the security guard's demeanor.

"Okay, Mr. Davidson. You can go up. Sorry about stopping you, but it's my job."

Bret nodded and pondered, "Mr. Davidson?"

He didn't say anything as he walked to the elevator. While Christmas music softly played in the elevator, he wondered what was going on. Were his expectations too high? When the elevator door opened, he walked toward the president's office.

"Mrs. DeBarry, I'm Bret Davidson. I have an—"

"Good morning, Mr. Davidson. Please go right in. Mr. Glassman is expecting you."

Mr. Davidson, he noticed again. No one had ever called him that before, and now two people had. He knocked at Mr. Glassman's door and went in.

"Bret, how are you doing this morning? Did you get much sleep last night?"

"Well, to be honest, I didn't sleep all that much. I guess I was just happy about getting back to work. How about you?"

"I slept like a baby. Best night's sleep I've had in years. You know, that guy, Harold, was so annoying at first, but I'm so glad he showed up the other night."

"That makes two of us. He certainly helped change my life. Speaking of which, Mr. Glassman, I'm wondering what you have in mind for me."

"First, I want to introduce you at the meeting. Bret, I've looked over your file. To be honest, I don't know how you slipped past me for all these years. I'm going to make you the chief operating officer of Glassman Industries, starting today. You'll report directly to me. No one else. What I'm saying is you're going to be second in command."

Bret almost collapsed. He had to sit down. "Mr. Glassman, I . . . I'm . . . overwhelmed that you have that kind of confidence in me after meeting me only two days ago. I think you need to reconsider. I . . . I . . . don't know if I can do that. To tell you the truth, I'd be happy just to work on the loading dock. I'm just happy to have a job."

"Nonsense! I've made the decision, and I'm going to follow through with it. If it's any consolation, I talked to Kacie about you, and she certainly thinks you have what it takes to do the job."

Bret couldn't believe it. Chief operating officer? Second in command?

"Sir, you realize I was breaking into your house to steal from you?"

Arnold responded softly, "You realize I was about to take my life. You risked going to jail to save my life. Besides, if I had gone through half of what you've been through recently, I would have done something crazy, too. And you and I both have someone in common, well, two people in common, including your Svengali and my healer, Harold. Somehow he brought us together."

Mrs. DeBarry interrupted their conversation. "Mr. Glassman, the department heads are waiting in the conference room."

"Thank you, I'm on my way. Come on, Bret."

The two walked into the conference room and took the two seats at the head of the table.

Bret saw his old boss, Dan Becton, looking very surprised and trying not to make eye contact with him. Bill McCarty, however, didn't look surprised. He looked shocked.

"Thank you for meeting with me this morning. I know this is a departure from our usual weekly meetings. But I'd like to introduce you to the new chief operating officer for Glassman Industries, Bret Davidson."

Becton coughed and sputtered, and McCarty turned pale.

"Bret is now the second highest officer of the company, and he will answer directly to me. All of you will now report to him. He and I will be working closely together over the next several months to rejuvenate the company. I expect things to pick up, and I plan to rehire all the people who were recently let go. I sincerely regret that decision and will try to make it up to them. In the meantime, if there are any short-term needs, I want those people to get first consideration. Well, this is the only thing on the agenda this morning. Let's make this a great day at Glassman's. I appreciate everything that all of you do. I can't thank you sufficiently enough for your service and your dedication to the company."

The department heads were stunned by the news and by the president's openness. Arnold Glassman had never spoken to them like this before, and he certainly had never said thank you for anything.

Bret, too, was still stunned by the news. While the heads all introduced themselves and congratulated him and indicated their willingness to work with him, two men held back. Rather than approach Bret, one of them focused on Arnold Glassman.

"Mr. Glassman," McCarty said. "Bret Davidson has never been anywhere close to this kind of responsibility. He's the least qualified person for COO! He doesn't even work here anymore! How can you do this? I plan to take this up with the board!"

But Arnold ignored him and gave Becton a look that would have melted steel. "Come with me, Bret. I want to show you to your new office."

It was second largest office in the building, close to Arnold's office. He had been saving it for the person who would eventually take over the company. Bret was speechless. This felt like a dream.

"How do you like it?" Arnold asked.

"It's amazing, Mr. Glassman. I'm overwhelmed."

"Well, I'm half sorry to say that your first order of business this morning is to fire someone."

"What? What did you say?"

"I said your first order of business is to fire someone."

"Who, who do you want me to fire?"

"I want you to fire Bill McCarty. As COO, you'll be taking over all of his responsibilities. And of course, you'll need an assistant to take some of the financial responsibilities off of you, but you'll be making the necessary decisions. Don't worry, I'll be working with you to show you the ropes and make sure you're comfortable before you start working without a net. Now, take care of that first matter. Make sure you tell him I'll work out his severance package."

"Okay, Mr. Glassman. I'll take care of it."

A moment after Arnold left him to settle into the office, Mrs. DeBarry appeared at his door. "Mr. Davidson, Mr. Glassman asked me to assist you until you hire an administrative assistant. Is there anything I can do for you?"

"Yes ma'am. Please ask Mr. McCarty to meet me in my office."

"Yes, of course. Right away."

"Mrs. DeBarry, is there any coffee around here?"

"I'll bring you a cup along with some papers Mr. Glassman wants you to look over."

Bret sat in his executive chair and looked straight ahead. He recalled the words of Pastor McDowell and Harold: "Maybe God is trying to get your attention or else He has something greater in store for you." He closed his eyes and mouthed, "Thank you, Lord."

Mrs. DeBarry returned with coffee and a file. Bret began looking through the file and sipping his coffee. A few moments later Bill McCarty knocked at his door.

"Come in," Bret said.

"You wanted to see me, Mr., uh, Mr. Davidson?"

Just as McCarty had done when he had summoned Bret to his office last week, the new COO didn't look up as he sipped his coffee. "Yes, please sit down."

Nervously, McCarty sat down, looking very perplexed.

"Well, Bill, this is a rough economy we're living in, and we're going to have to make some cutbacks and even terminate some people. Unfortunately, we're going to have to let you go," Bret said without looking up from the papers on his desk.

"What? You can't . . . you can't do that!"

"Mr. Glassman is finalizing your severance package per your contract. Please clean out your office in the next few minutes. Someone from security will escort you out of the building."

"Who do you think you are?" McCarty spewed venomously.

"I'm the chief operations officer, and I answer only to Mr. Glassman. Now, listen to me very carefully. I'll say it again very slowly. As Donald Trump used to say, 'you're fired!'"

McCarty stood in a huff and slammed the door on his way out.

Bret smiled. "I enjoyed that a little too much."

Chapter Eighteen

Mr. Davidson

Bret familiarized himself with everything Arnold sent his way. His day was flying by. And he was excited about his life and this new job. Occasionally, he needed to pinch himself to make sure it all wasn't a dream. Even though his world had changed dramatically in such a short time, he wanted to be sure he never became as arrogant and pompous as Bill McCarty had been as CFO. He needed to start a new trend for his position right away.

"Mrs. DeBarry," Bret said.

"Yes, Mr. Davidson."

"Would you ask Mr. Becton to come to my office?"

"Absolutely. Can I get you anything else? More coffee?"

"No ma'am, thank you for asking."

Bret walked to the window. He looked out and saw it had begun to snow. Christmas music quietly permeated

139

the executive offices. He looked at the company sign out front and shook his head as he thought how much last week, he never wanted to hear or see the name Glassman again. He certainly didn't mind the name Glassman now, especially in connection to Kacie.

Mrs. DeBarry intruded on his thoughts as she announced, "Mr. Becton is here to see you."

"Thank you, please send him in."

Becton looked extremely nervous as he entered Bret's office. Bret invited him to sit down.

"Do you know why I asked to see you, Dan?"

"I imagine you're going to fire me," he said as he lowered his head.

"That was my first thought," Bret paused. "But I've changed my mind."

Becton looked up, perplexed. Had he heard him correctly?

Bret said, "There's no need for me to remind you about what you did. What's done is done. But I want to tell you that I don't ever want you to do anything like that again to another employee of this company. I think you had a weak moment, and you were desperately trying to get ahead. I know you and your wife were expecting twins, and I know the additional time she spent in the hospital must have set you back financially, despite our hospitalization coverage. You desperately needed that promotion and the additional money. But don't ever do that to anyone else like you did to me."

Becton looked down and said, "I'm sorry, Bret . . . I mean, Mr. Davidson. You're right. I feel ashamed for presenting your ideas as my own. I'll never do anything like that again. Thank you for letting me keep my job. And just so you know, I felt terrible for what I did. Even with the promotion and the pay increase and our medical bills, my guilt has been eating me up inside. I know it doesn't mean much now, but can you forgive me?"

"We're all good, Dan. I hope you and your family have a wonderful Christmas!"

"Thank you, Bret, I mean, Mr. Davidson."

After Becton left, Bret called Kacie.

"Hello, Mr. Davidson!" she said with an excited voice.

"Hello, Miss Glassman!" he responded in kind.

"How's your day going with your new job?"

"Kacie, there's no way to describe how this day has gone. Your dad has been incredible to me. I feel so undeserving of all that I've been blessed with."

"Well, I don't think you're undeserving. I think my dad made the right decision. And by the way, I didn't have anything to do with his decision. He called me after looking over your HR file and after talking to some people you worked with in the office. I think he even contacted some of your professors."

"Really?" Bret said.

"Really!" she responded.

"Kacie, would you meet me for dinner? I have something to talk over with you if you have the time."

"I'd love to. Where would you like to eat?"

"How about O'Donnell's? At six?"

"I love that place. I'll see you at six!"

The afternoon flew by. When Bret noticed the last rays of the sun, he checked his watch and gathered his things. He paused to let Mrs. DeBarry know he was leaving.

"Thank you for all your help today, Mrs. DeBarry. You are a precious part of Glassman's. And I now know why Mr. Glassman thinks so highly of you."

"Thank you, Mr. Davidson. By the way, Joe Thomas asked if you would stop by the security desk on your way out."

Bret nodded as he walked out and into the hallway. The people still in their cubicles all smiled as he walked through the large work area. A couple gave him a little salute as he passed. He saluted back and smiled.

He had no idea why Joe wanted to see him. Maybe he felt he needed to apologize for his rudeness that morning. By now, Bret was walking on air and couldn't care less what the security officer had in mind.

Joe was on the phone as Bret approached him. He quickly ended his call and smiled when Bret entered his office.

"Hello, Mr. Davidson. I'm sorry about this morning. I was just doing my job. I meant no disrespect."

Bret responded, "No disrespect taken, Joe. Was that what you wanted to see me about?"

"No sir. I need to give you a new decal for your car and show you where your parking space is."

"Oh, well, thank you, Joe."

"I'll show you your new space."

Even in the parking garage the Glassman employees smiled and waved at him as the two men walked first to Bret's car, where Joe placed the decal on his back windshield, and then to the parking space right next to Arnold Glassman's parking space.

Bret shook Joe's hand and thanked him. When he drove out of the parking garage, he recalled passing Arnold's parking space the morning Joe had shown him the door and left his box on the sidewalk. This time, his eyes fell on the sign that read, "Reserved, Bret Davidson, COO." He shook his head, looked up, and said, "The hits just keep on coming."

CHAPTER NINETEEN

The Ring and the Question

Traffic was heavy, and for the first time, Bret noticed the Christmas lights along his drive. They were everywhere. He saw clusters of people with packages and homes brightened with Christmas glory. The city was overwhelmed with the wonderful spirit of Christmas.

When he arrived home, he went to his bedroom and pulled a box out of the closet. The box was full of pictures of his mom and dad. He looked at a few of them and tears came to his eyes. He pulled out a small jewelry box. When he opened it, his eyes lit up as he looked at his mother's ring.

The ring was beautiful, but it was very modest compared to the engagement rings Angie had long ago shown him. He put the box in his coat pocket and looked at the time. He had just enough time to get to the restaurant.

In the car, Bret turned up the radio to hear the song he had first heard at church a couple of days ago, "Mary Did You Know?"

Bret parked and entered the restaurant. He was surprised to see Angie there, but she wasn't a patron, she was the hostess. Amazingly, Bret didn't feel uncomfortable with seeing her, though she obviously was embarrassed to see him.

"Hello, Bret," she said cautiously. "Do you have a reservation?"

"Nice to see you, Angie. Yes, I have a reservation for two. Are you working here now?"

"Yes, I was let go by the firm," she said without making eye contact.

"I'm sorry to hear that."

"Thank you. You look good, Bret."

"Thanks, Angie. I couldn't be better."

Mercifully, Ed Harper, Bret's former cubicle mate, arrived to break the awkward moment. "Hey, Bret! Congratulations on your big promotion, brother. I'm so happy for you!"

"Thanks, Ed. Great to see you! I meant to pop by and say hello, but the time got away from me today."

Angie looked stunned. "You were promoted?"

"Yes. I'm the new chief operating officer of Glassman Industries. Today was my first day in the new position."

"Wow! COO. That's quite a promotion!"

"Yes, I'm very happy about it."

"Hello, Mr. Davidson," Kacie said from behind him.

"Hi, Kacie," Bret said and kissed her cheek. "Ed, this is Kacie. Kacie, this is Ed. He and I have worked together at Glassman's these last five years."

"Nice to meet, Ed," Kacie said.

"Nice to meet you too, Kacie. I hope you enjoy your meal," Ed said and turned to join his friends.

"I think our table's ready," Bret said, looking at Angie.

Bret's former fiancée looked totally dumbfounded as she grabbed a couple of menus. "Please follow me."

She showed them to the same table Bret and Angie were seated at the last time he saw Angie, the night she broke off their engagement. Angie gave them their menus and walked away sadly. Bret felt sorry for her.

"Well, Bret, how was your day?"

"Kacie, this has been an incredible day. I don't have the words to describe it. I had to pinch myself a couple of times just to be sure everything was real."

"I'm so happy for you, and I know you'll do a great job. My dad is very happy to have you. As a matter of fact, I can't remember the last time I saw my dad this happy."

"Speaking of happy," Bret started to say, taking a big breath, but all he could do after that was stutter. "Uh, I . . . well . . . I . . ."

"Are you okay?"

He took another breath and said, "Yes. I'm fine. I'm just a little nervous."

"Nervous about what?"

"Well, Kacie, I'm happy about the new position and getting to know your dad better, but I'm even happier about something else. The greatest thing that has ever happened to me is getting to know you."

Kacie smiled and blushed. She made eye contact with Bret and continued to smile. "I'm very happy about that, too, Bret. I had just about given up thinking I would ever meet someone like you."

"Really?" Bret said as he calmed down. "To be perfectly honest, if I had never gotten my job back but still found you, I would still be thrilled. You're the greatest thing that has ever happened to me. I know we've only known each other a short time, but I know I'm in love with you."

He reached in his coat pocket and pulled out the little box and placed it on the table in front of her. Kacie opened the box and saw the ring inside of it. Tears formed in her eyes and rolled down her cheeks.

"Kacie, this was my mom's ring. I know it's not a glamorous rock, but it means more to me than any ring I could ever find. I want to spend the rest of my life with you, if you'll have me. Kacie Glassman, will you marry me?"

She took the ring out of the box and placed it on her finger. It was a perfect fit.

"Bret, I'm in love with you, too. You couldn't have given me a more perfect ring than this one. I would love to marry you and spend the rest of our lives together."

Bret leaned over and kissed her. Several people at adjoining tables began to clap.

Kacie and Bret looked around and smiled as they held hands across the table.

"Kacie, if you don't mind, please don't say anything about this to your dad. I should have talked to him before I asked you. I know he would expect the man you marry to ask for his permission first."

"You got it!" Kacie said as she leaned over and kissed him again.

Bret said, "You know, all of this seems like a dream to me."

Chapter Twenty
Eggs and Milk

Harold was asleep, stretched across the couch. *It's a Wonderful Life* was on the television, and the movie was concluding with George Bailey reading the inscription from Clarence: "Thanks for the wings!"

"Harold! Harold! Wake up!" Marjorie said excitedly.

He opened his eyes in time to hear the little girl say, "Teacher says every time a bell rings, an angel gets his wings."

"What, what's going on?" Harold said with a confused look.

"Harold, I need you to go to the store and get a dozen eggs and a gallon of milk."

"What?" he said, still dazed from his nap. "I'm not married! I'm in heaven!"

"So you're saying it would be heaven to be single again—after twenty-eight years of marriage?"

"No, no. I was just dreaming. Wow! That was some realistic dream."

"Well, put your coat on. It's cold outside. And get me a dozen eggs and a gallon of milk if you want me to make your favorite Christmas cake. You better hurry, the kids are coming over."

Harold put on his coat and got in his car. Snowflakes were falling as he backed out of the driveway and headed to the store. Christmas music played on the radio.

When he stopped at a traffic light, he watched a wedding party emerge from a church. He couldn't believe his eyes. The just-married couple looked like Bret and Kacie from his dream. Then Kacie turned and hugged a man who looked just like Arnold Glassman.

Harold rubbed his eyes and said, "That was some dream," as the driver behind him blew his horn.

Harold continued to the grocery store. As he was about to go in, a bearded man dropped a package and bent over to pick up his things. Harold stopped to help him.

"Thanks, Harold," the man said as he walked away.

"How did you know my name?" he asked with a look of surprise.

When the man turned around, Harold saw it was Peter!

The old gentleman gave him a wink and vanished amid the snowflakes.

Acknowledgments

In September 1973, God reached from heaven and changed the heart of a broken young man. Thank you for your marvelous salvation through Jesus Christ, my Lord.

I want to thank the Legacy Adults at First Baptist Orlando for cheering me on during my time with them. Your encouragement will always be remembered.

Thank you to my girls, who have always been an inspiration in everything I have written.

Thank you Joe Sisto in Montreal for your patience, kindness, and understanding. You are an amazing lawyer, producer, and friend.

Thank you to Cliff McDowell in Toronto. You took a little book by an old professional wrestler and made it into a movie. Had you not believed in me, I would probably have stopped writing.

I want to thank Morgan James Publishing and the great staff there for believing in me again. They did an unbelievable job on my first book, *The Masked Saint.*

Working with them again on *Harold's Heavenly Christmas* has been a great joy.

I would especially like to thank David Hancock, the founder and CEO of Morgan James Publishing. He *is* the reason I chose to work with MJP.

I also want to thank Ed Curtis, who edited and made some great suggestions in helping *Harold's Heavenly Christmas* come to life. His help was invaluable.

And finally I would like to thank Dr. Jess C. Moody. In 1973, you held my future in the palm of your hand. Your encouragement then made all the difference in the world.

About the Author

Chris Whaley wrestled professionally from 1978 to 1988 as The Saint. He became a pastor in 1978 after graduating from Southwestern Baptist Theological Seminary. After he had been a pastor for a while, he realized he approached ministry in a different way than most pastors. It inspired him to write his first book, *The Masked Saint*.

In 2015, *The Masked Saint* was adapted as a feature film and released in January 2016. It received four nominations at the 2015 International Christian Film Festival (Best Actor, Best Director, Best Picture, and Best Musical Score) and was chosen as Best Picture.

Chris is a graduate of Palm Beach Atlantic University and Southwestern Baptist Theological Seminary. For forty-two years, he has served churches in Florida, and since June 2014, he has been on the staff of First Baptist Orlando.

He and his wife, Verna, have two daughters, Alyson and Kacie, and six grandchildren.